why she had provided him with the answer.

"I suppose that makes you the damsel in distress," he said.

"I'd like to think it makes me the knight."

"Sorry, darling," he said. "I kissed you awake not eight hours ago. That makes you the damsel."

"If we're going on fairy tales then that should make you Prince Charming, not the dragon."

He chuckled. "Sadly this is real life, not a fairy tale. And very often the Prince can be both."

*Three innocents encounter forbidden temptation
in this enticing new fairy-tale trilogy
by* New York Times *bestselling author Maisey Yates...*

Once Upon a Seduction...

Belle, Briar and Charlotte have lived sheltered lives,
far from temptation—but three billionaires are
determined to claim them!

Belle has traded herself for her father's freedom—
but the dark-hearted Prince keeping her prisoner
threatens to unleash an unknown sensuality...

Meanwhile Briar awakens to find herself abducted
by Prince Felipe—who blackmails her
into becoming his royal bride...

And Charlotte is reunited with the billionaire who
once climbed a tower to steal her innocence—and
Rafe is about to discover the secret consequences!

Find out if these young women can tame their
powerful men—*and* have their happily-ever-after!

The Prince's Captive Virgin
June 2017

The Prince's Stolen Virgin
August 2017

The Italian's Pregnant Prisoner
October 2017

THE PRINCE'S STOLEN VIRGIN

BY
MAISEY YATES

MILLS & BOON

First Published in Great Britain 2017
By Mills & Boon, an imprint of HarperCollins*Publishers*
1 London Bridge Street, London, SE1 9GF

© 2017 Maisey Yates

ISBN: 978-0-263-92454-1

Our policy is to use papers that are natural, renewable and recyclable
products and made from wood grown in sustainable forests. The logging
and manufacturing processes conform to the legal environmental
regulations of the country of origin.

Printed and bound in Spain
by CPI, Barcelona

Maisey Yates is a *New York Times* bestselling author of more than fifty romance novels. She has a coffee habit she has no interest in kicking, and a slight Pinterest addiction. She lives with her husband and children in the Pacific Northwest. When Maisey isn't writing she can be found singing in the grocery store, shopping for shoes online and probably *not* doing dishes. Check out her website: maiseyyates.com.

For my mom and dad, who read to me always
and made me fall in love with books—
most especially fairy tales—from the beginning.

My favorite stories always ended with
"they lived happily ever after." And they still do.

CHAPTER ONE

Once upon a time...

BRIAR HARCOURT MOVED quickly down the street, wrapping her long wool coat more tightly around her as the autumn breeze blew down Madison Avenue and seemed to whip straight on through to her bones.

It was an unseasonably cold fall, not that she minded. She loved the city this time of year. But there was always a strange sense of loss and nostalgia that mixed with the crisp air, and it was difficult for her to figure out what it was.

It would hover there, on the edges of her consciousness, for just a moment. Then it would slip away, like a leaf on the wind.

It was something to do with her life before she'd come to New York; she knew that. But she'd only been three when she'd been adopted by her parents, and she didn't remember her life before them. Not really. It was all impressions. Smells. Feelings. And a strange ache that settled low in her stomach.

Strange, because she loved her parents. And she loved her city. There shouldn't be an ache. You couldn't miss something you didn't even remember.

And yet, sometimes, she did.

Briar paused for a moment, a strange prickling sensation crawling up the back of her neck. It wasn't the cold. She was wearing a scarf. And anyway, it felt different. Different than anything she had ever experienced before.

She paused then turned around. The crowd behind her parted for a moment and she saw a man standing there. She knew, immediately, that he was the reason for the prickling sensation. He was looking at her. And when he saw that she was looking back, a slow smile spread over his face.

And it was like the sun had come out from behind the clouds.

He was beautiful. She could see that from here. Dark hair pushed back from his forehead, making him look carelessly windswept. There was dark stubble on his jaw, and something in his expression, in his eyes, that suggested he was privy to a host of secrets she could never hope to uncover.

He was… Well, he was a man. Nothing like the boys that she had been exposed to either at school or at various functions put on by her parents. Christmas parties at their town house, summer gatherings in the Hamptons.

He wouldn't stumble around, bragging about conquests or his beer pong score. No, never. Of course, she also wouldn't be allowed to talk to him.

To say that Dr. Robert Harcourt and his wife, Nell, were old-fashioned was an understatement. But then, she was their only child, and she had come to them late in life. Not only were they part of a different generation than many of her friends' parents, they had always made it very clear that she was precious to them. An unexpected gift they had never hoped to receive.

That always made her smile. It made the ache go away.

It didn't feel like a chore to do the best she could for them. To do her best to be a testament to all they'd put into raising her. She had always done her very best to make sure they were happy they'd made that decision. She'd tried—so very hard—to be the best she could be. To be perfect.

She had done her deportment lessons and her etiquette. Had done the debutante balls—even though it hadn't appealed to her at all. She had gone to school close to home, had spent every weekend back with her parents so they wouldn't worry. She'd never even considered rebelling. How could you rebel against people who had chosen you?

Except, right now, she felt a little bit like disregarding their concern. Like moving toward that man, who was still looking at her with those wicked eyes.

She blinked, and just as suddenly as he had appeared he was gone. Melted back into the crowd of black and gray coats. She felt an unaccountable sense of loss. A feeling that she had just missed something important. Something extraordinary.

You wouldn't know if it could have been extraordinary. You've never even kissed a man.

No. A side effect of that overprotectiveness. But then, she had no desire to kiss Tommy Beer Pong or his league of idiot friends.

Tall, sophisticated-looking men on bustling streets were another matter. Apparently.

She blinked then turned back around, heading back in the direction she had originally been going. Not that she was in a hurry. She was on break from school, and spending the days wandering her parents' town house wasn't terribly appealing. So she had decided she was going to go to the Met today, because she never got tired of wandering those halls.

But suddenly, the Met, and all the art inside, seemed lackluster. At least, in view of the man she had just seen.

Ridiculous.

She shook her head and pressed on.

"Are you running away from me?"

She stopped, her heart slamming against her breast-bone. Then she whirled around and nearly ran into the object of her thwarted feelings. "No," she said, the word coming out on a breath.

"You seemed to be walking quickly, and with great purpose."

Oh, his *voice*. He had an accent. Spanish, or some-thing. Sexy and like the sort of thing her brain would weave out of thin air late at night when she was trying to sleep, concocting herself the perfect mystery dream date that she would likely never find.

He was even better-looking up close. Stunning, even. He smiled, revealing perfect teeth. And then, he relaxed his mouth. There was something even more compelling about that. About being able to examine the shape of his lips.

"I wasn't," she said. "I just…" Somebody bumped into her as they walked by quickly. "Well, I didn't want to be in the way," she said, gesturing after the person, as if to prove her point.

"Because you had stopped," he pressed. "To look at me?"

"You were looking at *me*."

"Surely you must be used to that."

Hardly. At least, not in the way that he meant. Nobody likes to be different, and she was different in a great many ways. She was tall, first of all. Which was one refreshing thing about him. He was at least five inches taller than her height of five eleven, which was a rare and difficult thing to come across.

But yes, that was her. Tall. Skinny. All limbs. Plus, her hair was never going to fall in the effortless, silken waves most of her friends possessed. It took serious salon treatments to get it straight and she often questioned if it was worth it. Though, her mother insisted it was.

She was the opposite of the typical blonde beauty queen in her sorority or at any of the private schools she had attended growing up.

She stood out. And when you were a teenager, it was the last thing you wanted.

Though, now that she was in her early twenties, she was beginning to come to terms with herself. Her first instinct still wasn't to assume someone was staring because they liked what they saw. No, she always assumed they were staring because she was out of place.

"Not especially," she said, because it was honest.

"I don't believe that," he said. "You're far too beautiful to walk around not having men snap their necks trying to get a look."

Her face grew warm, her heart beginning to beat faster, harder. "I'm not really… I'm not supposed to talk to strangers."

That earned her a chuckle. "Then perhaps we should make sure to become something other than strangers."

She hesitated. "Briar. My name is Briar."

A strange expression crosssed his face, though it was fleeting. "A nice name. Different."

"I suppose it is." She knew it was. Yet another thing that made her feel like she stood out.

"José," he said, extending his hand.

She simply stared at it for a moment, as if she wasn't quite sure what he intended her to do. But of course she did know. He wanted to shake her hand. That wasn't weird. It was what people did when they met. She sucked in a sharp breath and allowed her fingers to meet his.

It was like she'd been hit by lightning. The electricity was so acute, so startling, that she immediately dropped his hand, taking a step back. She had never felt anything like that before in her life. And she didn't know if she wanted to feel it again.

"I have to go."

"No, you don't," he said, insistent.

"Yes. I do. I was on my way to… I was just going to… to a hair appointment." A lie easily thought of because she'd just been pondering her hair. But she could hardly tell him she was going to the museum. He might offer to walk with her. Though she supposed he could offer to take her to a salon, too.

"Is that so?"

"Yes. I have to go." She turned away, walking away from him quickly.

"Wait! I don't even know how to get in touch with you. At least give me your phone number."

"I can't." For a whole variety of reasons, but mostly because of the tingling sensation that still lingered on her hand.

She turned again, taking too-long strides away from him.

"Wait!"

She didn't. She kept on walking. And the last thing she saw was a bright yellow taxi barreling down on her.

* * *

Warmth flooded her. The strangest sensation assaulted her. Like she was being filled with oxygen, her extremities beginning to tingle. She felt disembodied, like she was floating in a dark space.

Except then it wasn't so dark. There was light. Marble walls. White. With ornate golden details. It was so clear. A place she'd never seen before, and yet…she must have.

Slowly, ever so slowly, she felt like she was being brought back to herself.

First, she could wiggle her fingertips. And then, she became aware of other things. Of the source of the warmth.

Lips against hers. She was being kissed.

Her eyes fluttered open, and in that instant she recognized the dark head bent over hers.

The man from the street.

The street. She had been crossing the street.

Was she in the street still? She couldn't remember leaving it. But she felt… Tied down.

She opened her eyes wider, looking around. There was a bright, fluorescent light directly above her, monitors all to her side. And she was tethered to something.

She curled her fingers into a fist and felt a sharp, stinging sensation.

She looked down at her arm and saw an IV.

And then, all her focus went straight back to the fact that she was still being kissed. In a hospital bed, presumably.

She put her hand up, her fingers brushing against his cheek, and then he pulled away.

"*Querida*, you're awake." He looked so relieved. Not

like a stranger at all. But then, he was kissing her, which was also unlike a stranger.

"Yes. How long was I…? How long was I asleep?" She posed the question to the nurse that she noticed standing just behind him. It was weird that he had kissed her. And she was going to get to that in a moment. But first she was trying to get a handle on how disoriented she felt.

"You were unconscious. Only for an hour or so."

"Oh." She pushed down on the mattress, trying to sit up.

"Now be careful," he said. "You might have a concussion."

"What happened?"

"You crossed the street right in front of a taxi. I was unable to stop you."

She vaguely remembered him calling after her, and her continuing to walk on. Feeling slightly frantic as she did. Logically, she knew that her parents were overprotective. She knew that they had been hypervigilant in instilling the concept of stranger danger to her, but she had taken it on board, even knowing that it was a little bit over the top.

They had told her that she had to be particularly careful because Robert was a high-profile physician who often worked with politicians and helped write legislation pertaining to the healthcare system, and that made him something of a target. She had to be extra vigilant because of that, and because of the fact that they were wealthy.

It had made her see the bogeyman in any overly friendly stranger on the street as a child, but she supposed it had kept her safe. Until she had met *him* and run out in front of a car.

Her parents. She wondered if anyone had called them. They wouldn't be expecting her home until evening.

"Excuse me…" But the nurse had rushed out of the room, presumably to get a doctor? She didn't know why the woman hadn't stopped to check her vitals.

"My father is a doctor," she said, looking back up at José. That was his name. That was what he had said his name was.

"That is good to know," he said, a slight edge in his voice that she hadn't heard earlier.

"If he hasn't been called already, somebody should get in touch with him. He's going to want input on my treatment."

"I'm sorry," José said, straightening.

Suddenly, his face looked different to her. Sharper, harder. Her heart thundered dully, a strange lick of fear moving through her body.

"You're sorry about what?"

"It isn't going to be possible for your father to have input on your treatment. Because you're going to be moved."

"I am?"

"Yes. It seems to me that you are stable, and that has been confirmed by my nurse."

"Your nurse?"

He sighed heavily, lifting his hand and checking his watch. Then he adjusted the cuff on his jacket, the mannerism curt and officious. "Yes. My nurse," he said, sounding exasperated as though he was explaining something to a small child. "You do not have to worry. You will be treated by my doctor once we arrive in Santa Milagro."

"Where is that? I don't understand."

"You don't know where Santa Milagro is? I do question the American school system in that case. It is truly a shame that you had to be brought up here, Talia."

Something niggled at her, something strange and steep. As deep as those wistful feelings she often felt when the air began to cool. "My name isn't Talia."

"Right. Briar." His smile took on a sardonic twist. "My mistake."

"The fact that I don't know where Santa Milagro is is not the biggest issue we have. The biggest issue is that I'm not going to see your doctor. You're just a crazy man that I met on the street. For all I know you stole that coat—it is a really nice coat—and you're actually an insane vagrant."

"A vagrant? No. Insane? Well. That matter is fully up for debate. I won't lie."

"José—"

"My name isn't José. I'm Prince Felipe Carrión de la Viña Cortez. And you, my dear Briar, are mine by rights. I have spent a great many years looking for you, and now I have finally found you. And you're coming with me."

CHAPTER TWO

PRINCE FELIPE CARRIÓN DE LA VIÑA CORTEZ had yet to lose
sleep over any of his actions. As long as he steered clear
of covert murders to further his political status, he was
better than his father.

A low bar, certainly. But Felipe liked a low bar. They
were so much easier to step over.

And while this might be the lowest he'd stooped, it
was also going very well. Surely if he wasn't supposed
to have Princess Talia she wouldn't have delivered herself quite so beautifully to him.

Well, the part where she was hit by a taxi was perhaps
not ideal, but it had certainly made the second half of his
scheme easier. Because she was now confined to a hospital bed, being wheeled through an empty corridor—
something he was pleased he'd arranged, because she
was yelling for help, and it was much nicer to not have to
deal with anyone trying to come to her aid—and he was
going to have her undergo a quick check by a privately
hired physician before having her loaded onto the plane.

He was covering all his bases, and truly, being quite
generous.

Though he supposed the kiss hadn't been wholly necessary. But remembering the way she had jolted when

she'd seen him on the street, he had wondered. Wondered if there was enough electricity between them to shock her awake.

It had worked, apparently.

Other men might feel some guilt over kissing an unconscious woman. Not this man.

Not with this woman.

She was owed to him. Owed to Santa Milagro. She should be thankful that he was the one who had found her. Had it been his father…

Well. Yet more reasons Felipe would be losing no sleep over this. Life with him would be a kindness by comparison.

Though it was clear to him that his princess did not see it now.

"Are you insane?" She was still shouting, and he was becoming bored with it.

"As previously mentioned, it is entirely possible that I'm crazy. However, hurling it around like an epithet is hardly going to help."

She looked up at him, her dark eyes blazing, the confusion from earlier cleared from them. Even now—in a hospital gown—she was beautiful. Though her rich skin tone would be better served in golds, colors like gems. Not the sallow, white and blue cloth her slight curves were currently covered by.

No, he would see her dressed like a queen, which she soon would be. His queen. Once his father died and Felipe assumed the throne.

He had a feeling his father would be distinctly unhappy to know that Felipe had managed to track down the quarry his father had spent so many years searching for. Good thing the old bastard was bound to his bed.

Though, even if he was not, Felipe had the support of the people, and at this point, the support of the military. He supposed considering treason in the form of dispatching his own father was probably not the best course of action.

Though, if the old man was healthier, the likelihood of him considering it would be much higher.

There would be no need to do that. No. Instead, he would bring Talia back to the palace, and he would parade her before his father like a cat might deliver a bird to its master. Except the old king was not Felipe's master. Not anymore.

He passed the nurse a large stack of US dollars after she helped load the princess into the back of the van he had hired. He would not be paying anyone with anything traceable. No. He wanted all of this to go off without a ripple in the media.

Until he decided to make the tidal wave.

This would be one of his grandest illusions, and he was a master of them. Sleight of hand and other trickery so that he would be consistently underestimated on the world stage. Because it suited him. It suited him endlessly.

Well, that wasn't true. The end was coming.

Talia was a means to it.

"To the airport," he said to his driver as the van was secured.

"The airport?" She was sounding quite shrill now.

"Well, we aren't swimming to Santa Milagro. Not in your condition, anyway."

"I am not going with you."

"You are. Though I appreciate your spirit. It's admirable. Particularly given that you're currently in a hospital bed. I will have you undergo a preliminary examination before we get on the plane."

The physician he'd hired moved from his seat over to where Talia was. He proceeded to examine her, taking her blood pressure, looking at her eyes. "You may want to order a CT scan once you get back to your country," the older man said. If he was feeling any compunction about being involved in this kidnapping, he was hiding it well.

But, considering the amount of money that Felipe was throwing at him, he should hide it well.

"Thank you. I will make sure she has follow-up appointments. I do not want her broken, after all."

She did not look relieved by that news, though in his opinion she should.

"If you have any integrity at all," she said, reaching out and grabbing the doctor by the arm, "then you'll tell somebody where I am. Who I'm with."

The older man looked away from her, clearly uncomfortable, and withdrew his arm.

"Talia," Felipe said, "he has been paid too well to offer you any help."

"You keep calling me Talia. And I'm not Talia. I don't know who Talia is."

Well, that was certainly an interesting development. "Whether or not you know who Talia is—and that I question—you are her."

"I think maybe you're the one who hit your head," she said.

"Again, sadly for you, I did not. While I may not be of sound mind, I certainly know my own mind. This... Well, this has been planned for a very long time. You think it accidental that I encountered you on a busy street in New York City? Of course not. The most random of encounters are always carefully orchestrated."

"By some sort of higher power?" she asked, her tone wry.

"Yes. Me."

"I have no idea who you are. I have never heard of you, I have never heard of your country, so I can only imagine that it is the size of a grain of rice on a world map. While we're talking size, I can only assume that plays a factor in a great many things, since you seem to be compensating."

He chuckled. "If I were not so secure I might be offended by that, *querida*. Anyway, while I am a believer in the idea that size matters in some arenas, when it comes to world events, often the size of the country is not the biggest issue. It is the motion of the... Well, of the cash flow. The natural resources. And that, my country has in abundance. However, we are going through a few structural changes. You are part of those changes."

"How can I be part of those changes? I'm a doctor's daughter. I'm a university student. I don't have a place on the world stage."

"And that is where you're wrong. But we're not going to finish having this discussion here."

He had paid the good doctor for his silence, that much was true, but he did not trust anything when a larger payday had the potential to come into play. And when news of Briar Harcourt going missing hit the media, there was a chance that the man would go forward with his story.

That meant that the details revealed in the van needed to be limited. Soon, however, they arrived at the airport, and the vehicle pulled up directly to Felipe's private plane.

"Don't we have to go through customs? I don't have… Well, I don't have a passport."

"Darling. You're traveling with me now. I am your passport. Does she need the IV any longer?" He posed that question to the doctor.

"She shouldn't," came the grave reply.

"Then remove it," Felipe commanded.

The doctor did so, carefully and judiciously, putting a Band-Aid over where the needle had been.

"She is not hooked up to anything else?"

"No," the doctor replied.

"Excellent." Felipe reached down, wrapping his arms around Talia and hoisting her up out of the bed. "Good help is all very well and good, but in the end it's always better to do things yourself."

She clung to him for a moment, clearly afraid of falling out of his arms and getting another head injury, and continued to hold on to him while he got out of the van and began to stride across the tarmac toward the plane.

And then she began to struggle.

"Please do not make this difficult," he said, tightening his hold on her, not finding this difficult at all, though he would rather not end up with a bruise if it could be helped. If he was going to be marred, he preferred for it to happen in the bedroom. At least then, there would be a reward for his suffering.

Hell, sometimes the suffering was just part of the reward.

"The point is to make this difficult!"

"I have never had a woman resist getting on my private plane quite so much."

"But you've had them resist. That says nothing good about you."

He sighed heavily, taking them both up the steps and into the aircraft. His flight crew immediately mobilized, closing the door and beginning the process of readying for takeoff. As they had been instructed prior to his and the princess's boarding.

"You say that as though it should bother me," he said, setting her down in one of the plush leather chairs on the plane before sitting down in the chair across from her. "Don't bother to try and get up and unlock the door. It can only be unlocked from the cockpit now. I made arrangements for some high-security additions to be added to the plane before coming to get you."

"That seems stupid," she said. "What if we need to get out and the pilots can't let us out?"

He chuckled, reluctantly enjoying the fact that she seemed so comfortable running her mouth even though she had absolutely no power in the situation. "Well, I can actually control it from my phone, as well. But don't get any ideas about trying to do it yourself. It requires fingerprint and retina recognition."

"Fine. But if the plane catches fire and we need to get out and somehow your fingerprints have melted off and you can't open your eyes and we die a painful death because of your security measures…"

"Well," he said. "In such a case I will feel terribly guilty. And, I imagine continue the burning in hell."

"That's a given."

"Are you concerned for the state of my eternal soul?"

"Not at all. I'm concerned for the state of my present body." She looked around, and he could tell the exact moment she realized she had nothing. That she was wearing a hospital gown, that she had no identification, no money and no phone.

"I do not intend to harm you," he said, reaching down and straightening his cuffs. "In fact, that runs counter to my objective."

"Your objective is to...improve my health?"

"Does it need improving? Because if it does, I most certainly will."

"No," she laid her head back, grimacing suddenly. "Okay. Well, right now it needs slight improvement because I feel like I was hit by a taxi." She sat upright, slamming her hands down on either side of her, her palms striking the leather hard, the sound echoing in the cabin. "Oh, yes! Because I was hit by a taxi!"

"Regrettable. While I orchestrated a great many things, that was not one of them. I would never take such a risk with you."

"Maybe now is a good time for you to explain yourself. Since we've established I'm not going anywhere. And I assume that Santa Milagro is not a quick and easy flight. I suppose we have the time."

"In a moment." The engines fired up on the plane, and they began to move slowly. "I like a little atmosphere. And I don't want to be interrupted by takeoff."

The aircraft began to move faster and he reached across to the table beside him, opening the top and pressing a button. An interior motor raised a shelf inside, delivering a bottle of scotch, along with a tumbler.

As the plane began to ascend he opened the bottle and poured himself a generous measure of the amber liquid. He did not spill a drop. That would be a mistake. And he did not make mistakes.

Unless he made them on purpose.

"And now?" she pressed.

"Do you want to change first?" He took a sip of his drink. "Not that the hospital gown isn't lovely."

Her face contorted with rage. "I don't care what I'm wearing. And I really don't care what you think of it."

"That will change. I guarantee it."

"You don't know very much about women, do you?"

He set his glass down on the table. "I know a great deal about women. Arguably more than you do."

"You don't know anything about this woman. I don't know what kind of simpering idiots you normally capture and drag onto your plane, but I'm not impressed by your wells, by your title, by your power. My father did not raise a simpering, weak-willed idiot. And my mother did not raise a fool."

"No, indeed. However, they were raising a princess."

"I'm not a princess."

"You are. The Princess of Verloren. Long-lost. Naturally."

"That is… That is ridiculous."

"It is the subject of a great many stories, a great many films… Wouldn't you think that something like that, a story so often told, might have its roots in reality?"

"Except this isn't *The Princess Diaries* and you are not Julie Andrews."

He chuckled. "No, indeed." He took another sip of his scotch. Funny, alcohol didn't even burn anymore. Sometimes he missed it. Sometimes he simply assumed it was a metaphor for his conscience and found amusement in it. "A cursory internet search would corroborate what I'm telling you. King Behrendt and Queen Amaani lost their only daughter years ago. Presumed dead. The entire nation mourned her passing. However, in Santa

Milagro it was often suspected the princess had been sent into hiding."

"Why would I be sent into hiding?"

"Because of an agreement. An agreement that your father made with mine. You see, sometime after the death of his first wife, the king fell on hard times. His own personal mourning affected the country and led the nation to near financial ruin. And so he borrowed heavily from my father. He also promised that he would repay my father in any manner he deemed acceptable. He more than promised. It is in writing." Felipe lifted a shoulder then continued, "Of course, at the time King Behrendt felt like he had nothing to lose. His wife was dead. His heir and spare nearly grown. Then he met a model. Very famous. Originally from Somalia. Their romance stunned all of Europe for a great many reasons, the age gap between them being one of them."

"I know this story," she said, her voice hushed. "I mean, I have heard of them."

"Naturally. As they are one of the most photographed royal couples in the world. What began as a rather shocking coupling has become one of the world's favorites."

"You're trying to tell me that they are my parents."

"I'm not *trying* to tell you that. I *am* telling you that. Because when it came time to collect on the king's debt… My father demanded you."

"He did?"

"Oh, yes. Verloren, and indeed the world, was captivated by your birth. And when you finally arrived, a great party was given. Many gifts were brought from rulers all over the world. And my father—not in attendance because he was any great friend of yours, but because your father was obligated—came, but it was not with a gift. It was a promise. That when you were of age he would come for you. And that you would be his wife."

Her skin dulled, her lips turning a dusky blue. "Are you… Are you taking me to your father? Is that what this is?"

He shook his head. "No. I am not delivering you to my father. For that, you should be thankful. You will not be his wife."

"No," she said firmly. "I will not be."

He looked up at her then, his eyes meeting hers. She looked fiery, determined. Anger glittered in those ebony depths, and perversely he ached to explore that rage. Sadly, it would have to wait.

"You will not be my father's wife," he repeated, pausing for just a moment. "You will be mine."

CHAPTER THREE

SHE LOST CONSCIOUSNESS after that. And really, she was somewhat grateful for that. Less so when she woke up feeling disoriented, cocooned in a bed of soft blankets in completely unfamiliar surroundings.

At least when she woke up this time it wasn't because he had kissed her.

Though, he was standing on the far side of the room, his arms crossed over his broad chest, his expression one of dark concern. Perhaps that was an odd characteristic to assign to concern, but she had a feeling the concern wasn't born out of any kind of goodness of his heart, rather over the potential thwarting of his schemes.

His schemes to make her his wife. She remembered that with a sudden jolt.

She sat up quickly, and her head began to throb.

"Be careful, Princess," came a slow, calming voice. "You do not have a concussion, but you have certainly been through quite a lot in the past twenty-four hours."

She became aware that a woman was standing to the left of her bed. A woman who had that kind of matter-of-fact bedside demeanor she typically assigned to physicians.

"Are you a doctor?" she asked.

"Yes. When you lost consciousness on the flight, Prince Felipe called and demanded that I make myself available to him as soon as the plane landed. I told him it was likely stress and a bit of dehydration that caused the event." She sent him a look that carried not a small amount of steel.

"I have indeed been placed under stress," Briar said. "Since he kidnapped me."

The woman looked like she was about to have an apoplexy. "Kidnapped. Lovely."

"Did you have a criticism, Dr. Estrada?" Felipe asked, his tone soft but infinitely deadly.

"Never, Your Majesty."

"I thought not."

"Perhaps you ought to criticize him," Briar said.

"Not if she would like to retain her license to practice medicine here in Santa Milagro. Also, not as long as she would like to stay out of the dungeon."

"He would not throw me in the dungeon," Dr. Estrada said, her tone hard. "However, I do believe he might strip me of my license."

"Do not think me so different from my father," he said, his tone taking on a warning quality. "I will have to assume control of the country soon, and I will do whatever I must to make sure that transition goes as smoothly as possible. I would like to give you all that I have promised," he said, directing those words to the doctor, "but I cannot if you don't help me in this. I am not evil like my father, but I am entirely focused on my goals. I will let nothing stand in my way." He rolled his shoulders backward, grabbed the edge of his shirtsleeve and pulled it down hard. "I am hardly a villain, but I am...morally flexible. You would both do well to remember that."

"You can't exactly issue threats to me," Briar said, "as I've already been kidnapped."

"Things can definitely get worse," Felipe said, a sharp grin crossing his lips. "I'm quite creative."

A shiver ran down her back and she thought wildly about what she could do. There was no hope of running, obviously. She wasn't feeling her best, even if she didn't have a concussion. She was also stranded in a foreign country with no ID, no money, nothing but a hospital gown.

"Help me," she said to Dr. Estrada, because she had no idea what else she could do.

"I'm afraid I can't," the woman said. "Except when it comes to your medical well-being. You can take a couple of these pain pills if you need them." She set the bottle on the nightstand.

"I might take the whole thing," Briar responded.

"I will not tolerate petulant displays of insincere overdoses." Felipe walked across the room, curling his fingers around the pill bottle and picking it up. "If you need something I am more than happy to dispense it. Or rather, I will entrust a servant to do so."

He was appalling. It was difficult to form an honest opinion on his personality, given that he had kidnapped her and all. That was the dominant thing she was focused on at the moment. But even without the kidnap, he was kind of terrible.

"That will be all, Dr. Estrada," he said, effectively dismissing what might have been Briar's only possible ally. "She would not have helped you," Felipe said, as if reading her mind. "She can't. You see, my father has had this country under a pall for generations. People like Dr. Estrada want to make a difference once the old king is dead—and he is closer and closer to being dead with each passing moment we spend talking. I would prefer that he live for our marriage announcement, however. Still, if he does not, I won't lose any sleep over it. The sooner he dies, the better. The sooner he dies, the sooner I assume the throne. And change can begin coming to the country."

"There's nothing you can do until some old, incapacitated king dies?"

He waved a hand. "Of course there is. If there was nothing that could be done, Dr. Estrada wouldn't have been here at all. In fact, she's somebody that I've been meeting with for the past couple of years, getting a healthcare system in place, ready to launch the moment I assume power. I have pieces in a great many strategic places on this chessboard, Princess. And you were the last one. My queen."

"I don't understand."

"Of course you don't. But you will. Ultimately, this will benefit your country. Your parents."

"My parents live in New York," she said, gritting her teeth. "I don't care about anybody else."

He made a tsking sound. "That's quite heartless. Especially considering the king and queen assumed great personal cost to send you to safety."

"I might feel something more if I knew them," she said, ignoring the slight twinge of guilt in her chest. "As it is, I'm concerned that the mother and father I know are going to be frantic, looking for me."

"Likely they will be. But soon, very soon, I will be ready to announce to the world that we are engaged."

"And what's to keep me from flinging myself in front of the camera and letting everybody know that I'm not your fiancée, I'm a kidnap victim? And you are danger-ously delusional."

"Oh," he said, "you've got me there. Something I didn't think of. I've only been planning exactly how my ascendance to the throne would go for the past two de-cades. But here, you have completely stumped me with only a few moments of thinking." He laughed, the sound derisive. "Your country, your father's country, owes mine an astronomical amount. I could destroy them. Bankrupt them. The entire populace would spend the remainder of their days in abject poverty. A once great nation top-pled completely. I, and I alone, have been the only thing standing in the gap between my father and his revenge on Verloren. My own had to go neglected so that I could protect yours. I spent every favor on that. Used every ounce of diplomacy to convince him that it was not the time to move on Verloren. I placated him with ideas that I had gotten leads on your whereabouts." He shook his head. "I did a great deal to clinch this. If you think you're going to thwart me with a temper tantrum then you are truly delusional."

"Well, I was hit by a taxi."

He laughed again. "True. I should have given the driver a tip. He made this all that much easier. Anyway, you will be well taken care of here."

"I just have to marry a monster."

"There is that," he said, looking completely unfazed by the insult. "What sort of monster do you suppose I am, Princess?"

She couldn't tell if he was asking the question with sincerity. She wasn't sure she cared. But as she looked at him, a picture began to form in her mind. His eyes were gold, glinting with heat and the possibility of a kind of cruelty she didn't want to test. There was something sharp about him, whip-smart and deadly.

"A dragon. Clearly," she said, not entirely sure why she had provided him with the answer.

"I suppose that makes you the damsel in distress," he said.

"I'd like to think it makes me the knight."

"Sorry, darling," he said. "I kissed you awake not eight hours ago. That makes you the damsel."

"If we're going off fairy tales then that should make you Prince Charming, not the dragon."

He chuckled. "Sadly, this is real life, not a fairy tale. And very often the prince can be both."

"Then I suppose a princess can also be a knight. In which case, I would be careful, because when you go to kiss me again I might stab you clean through."

He lifted one dark brow. "Then the same goes for you. Because the next time I go to kiss you, I might decide to swallow you whole instead."

There was something darkly sexual about those words, and she resented the responses created in her body. No matter that he was... Well, insane almost by his own admission, he was still absurdly beautiful.

And that, she supposed, was ultimately what he meant about the dragon and the prince being one and the same. On the outside, he was every inch Prince Charming. From his perfectly tailored jacket and dark pants, to his classically handsome face and picture of exquisite masculinity that was his body.

But underneath, he breathed fire.

"I am announcing our engagement tomorrow. And you will not go against me."

"How do you know?"

"Because I'm going to allow you to call your parents tonight. At least, the people you know as your parents."

"They'll send someone for me. They'll contact that… They'll contact the president if they have to."

"They won't," he said, his voice holding an air of finality. "And you know why? Because they do know the whole story of how you came to be theirs. They know exactly who you are, and they know why they cannot interfere in this. They were charged with keeping you safe from me, and they failed. Now, there is nothing that can be done. Once you have passed into the possession of the dragon… Well. It is too late. Tell them everything that I told you. And they will confirm what I've said. You don't have a choice. Not if you want to keep your homeland from crumbling. Not if you ever hope to see things actually fixed. This is bigger than you. When you speak to them, you'll know that's the truth."

Then he turned, leaving her alone with nothing but a sense of quiet dread.

"I will be having an engagement party in the next week or so," Felipe said, staring fixedly out the window at the view of the mountains.

"That seems sudden," his friend Adam said on the other end of the phone.

Adam was recently married to his wife, Belle, after years of isolating himself on his island country, lost in grief after the death of his first wife, and hiding the terrible scars he had received from the accident that had made him a widower. But now things had changed. Since he had met Belle, he had come back into the public eye, and he seemed to have no issue with public appearances.

All the better as far as Felipe was concerned, because he wanted to have as much public support as possible.

"It isn't," Felipe said. "Believe me."

"Why do I get the feeling this is the sort of thing I don't want to know the details about?" his other friend Rafe said, his tone hard.

"You likely don't," Felipe said. "But I would happily give them to you. You know I have no shame."

He didn't. Though he was hardly going to engage in unbridled honesty and a heart-to-heart with his friends about the current situation. That wasn't how he worked. It wasn't the function he fulfilled in the group.

He'd cultivated the Prince Charming exterior long ago. Out of necessity. For survival. Image had been everything to his father, and the older man had always threatened Felipe and his mother with dire consequences if Felipe were to reveal the state of their lives in the palace.

The consequences of behaving otherwise were dire, and he had discovered that the hard way.

So he had learned, very early on, not to betray himself. Ever. He kept everything close to his chest, while appearing to give the whole world away.

"I would like details," Adam said, "before I know what sort of circus I'm bringing my pregnant wife to."

"Congratulations," Felipe said. "Please make the announcement before you come to my party. I don't want the impending arrival of your heir to overshadow my engagement."

"I suppose that's about all the sincerity I can expect out of you," Adam said, his tone dry.

"Probably. But you see, I have found a long-lost—presumed dead—princess. And, I'm making her my wife. This is good for me for more than one reason. All political things, I won't bore you with them. Suffice it to say, this party is going to be quite the affair."

"I see. And how exactly did you find this princess?"

"Well, there's an app. I just opened it up and trapped her inside a little ball."

Adam snorted. "I wish that were true, Felipe. But I have a feeling that a lot more skullduggery was involved."

"There was skullduggery. I cannot deny the existence of skullduggery. Ultimately, I consider that a good thing since skullduggery is a sadly underused word."

"I do not need details," Rafe said. "But is my support of you going to damage the value of the stock in my company? That, I do need to know."

"And I need to know if she is the princess of any country possessing nuclear weapons. Because again, my support cannot endanger my people," Adam added.

"If the actual details of how I came in to possession of the princess were released, it might in fact cause you both trouble. But they won't. First of all, her parents owe an astronomical amount of money to my country. As much as they might want to contest the marriage, they won't be able to. And, once she is more familiar with the situation, she will feel the same way."

"So, you're forcing her into marriage?" Adam asked.

"Do I detect a hint of judgment in your voice?" Felipe returned. "Because if I remember correctly you came into possession of your wife when you took her prisoner."

"That was different."

"How?"

"Because *I* did it," Adam said. "Plus, I wouldn't do it now."

"Because love has changed you and softened you. I understand. Sadly, I'm not looking for love." The very idea almost made him laugh. "No chance of softening. But I do believe that in the end this is going to be the best thing for Santa Milagro. If it isn't the best thing for one woman, when all of my people could be benefited, I have to say I'm going to side with my people."

"So," Rafe said, slowly. "You are asking us to attend your engagement party, where you will announce your intention to marry a woman that you kidnapped, who doesn't want to marry you, but who will have to pretend as though she does so that you don't bring terrible consequences down on her mother and father, and her entire country."

"Yes," Felipe said.

"That sounds about right," Rafe responded.

"My wife will be...unhappy," Adam said.

"Then don't tell her. Or, tell her that's how all the girls meet their husbands these days. Stockholm syndrome."

Adam growled. "I'm not going to keep it from her."

"Fine. But I do expect that she fall in line," Felipe said, having not considered that his friend's potential loose cannon of a spouse might be an issue. Who knew what Belle might say to the press?

"Belle does not *fall in line*," Adam said. "It isn't in her nature. However, I will explain the sensitive political situation. I know she would not wish to cause harm. And while I don't trust that you won't cause any harm, Felipe, I do trust you're trying to prevent greater harm."

"Of course. Because I'm an altruist like that. Details will be forthcoming, but of course I had to call and give you the good news myself."

"Because you're such a good friend," Rafe said, the words rife with insincerity.

No, the truth was, they were friends. True friends, the

kind that Felipe had never expected to have. The kind that, he imagined, had prevented him from becoming something entirely soulless.

They had some idea about his upbringing. About the way that he was. But mostly, he showed them the face he showed the world. Prince Charming, as he had just discussed with Talia.

The dragon, he kept to himself.

Usually.

CHAPTER FOUR

BRIAR WAS ABOUT to give in to despair when there was a knock on the door. She knew immediately that it wasn't Prince Felipe, as she had a feeling he didn't knock. Ever.

She was proven correct when a servant came through the door after she told her to come in.

"This phone is programmed so that you may call your parents," the woman said. "I will give you some privacy."

She turned and swept out of the room, leaving Briar there with the phone. The first thing she tried to do was call 911, which was stupid, because she knew that it wasn't an emergency number in Santa Milagro. The phone wasn't connected to the internet, so she couldn't search any other numbers, but she had a feeling that even if she could it was programmed to only connect to one other number.

She should dial them immediately. After all, except for when she was at school, this was the longest she'd gone without contact with them. And even when she'd been at university it had been…different. She'd been in an approved location, doing exactly what they'd asked her to do.

Right now she was…well, somehow rootless, even as she learned the truth of where she'd come from. On her own, in a way she never had been before, even while she was being held captive.

For one moment, she thought about not calling. It was a strange, breathless moment, followed by her stomach plummeting all the way to her toes, even as she couldn't believe she had—for one moment—considered something so selfish.

They were probably sick with worry. And it was her fault, after all. She was the one who had approached Felipe. She was the one who had opened herself up to this. She had failed them. After trying so hard for so much of her life to make sure she could be the daughter they deserved to have, now they were going through this.

With shaking fingers, she dialed her parents. And she waited.

It was her father who answered, his tone breathless in rush. "Yes?"

"It's me," she said.

"Briar! Thank God. Where are you? Are you okay? We've been searching. We called the police. We've called every hospital."

"I know," she said. "I mean, I knew you would have. But this is the first chance I've had to call. I wasn't…I've been kidnapped," she said. As much as she didn't want to cause her parents any alarm, kidnapped was what she was; there was no sugarcoating it.

Her father swore violently, and a moment later she heard the other line pick up. "Briar?" It was her mother.

"I'm okay. I mean, I'm unharmed. But I'm in…"

"Santa Milagro," her father said, his tone flat.

The world felt like it tilted to the side. "You know? How do you know?" He had told her they would. But she realized that up until that moment she truly hadn't believed him.

"Perhaps it was a mistake," her father said slowly, "to keep so much from you. But we saw no other way for you to have a normal, happy life. It wasn't our intention to keep your identity from you, not really. But we didn't know what kind of life you would have if you knew that you were a princess that couldn't live in a palace. If you knew that you had parents who had given birth to you across the world, who didn't want to give you up but had felt forced into it."

"It was selfish maybe," her mother said, her tone muted. "But your mother and father did agree. They agreed that it would be best if you knew only us. They agreed it would be best if you didn't feel split in your identity. But we all knew it couldn't go on forever. We simply hoped this wouldn't be the reason."

Briar felt dizzy. "Am I Talia? Princess Talia. That's what he keeps calling me. Is that true?"

"It is true." Her father said it with the tone of finality.

"How? How can everybody just keep something like this from me? This is my life! And yeah, you were always overprotective and everything, but I didn't realize it was because I was in danger of actually being kidnapped by some crazy prince from half a world away." She took a deep breath. "I didn't realize it was because I was…a princess."

It felt absurd to even think, let alone say.

"It lasted longer than we thought it would," her mother said, her voice soft. "And I can't say that I've been unhappy about it. You're all we have, Briar. And to us, that's who you are. Our daughter. We wanted so badly to protect you." She heard the other woman's voice get thick with tears. "We failed at that."

Briar felt…awash in guilt. A strange kind. They were distressed because of her. Because they had been embroiled in this and probably hadn't a clue what the best way to handle it was. Of course there wasn't exactly a parenting book called *So You Have to Keep an Endangered Princess Safe While Raising Her as Your Own*. It might hurt, to find all this out now, but she certainly couldn't blame them.

"He says I have to marry him," she said, her voice hushed.

"The king?"

"Prince Felipe," she said.

The sound of relief on the other end of the phone was audible. "At least he's not… His father is a devil," her father said. "That was why your birth parents, the king and queen, sent you away from your country. Because they knew a life with him would destroy you."

"I don't want to marry Felipe, either, though," she said. "I don't want to be a princess. I just want to go back home."

There was a pause. A silence that seemed to stretch all the way through her.

"I'm afraid that's impossible. Now that he has you… It would be catastrophic to your birth parents…if any of this were to get out. The money that was borrowed by Verloren. Because any business done with King Domenico would be considered a blight on your mother and father. They would never recover from it. And the consequences to the country would be severe if Santa Milagro decided that the terms of the deal had been violated. The national treasury would be drained. People would have nothing. No food, no housing. No healthcare."

As he spoke those words, she felt weight settling on her shoulders. A new one added with each thing he listed would be denied to the citizens of her home country—a home country she couldn't even find on a map—if she chose not to comply.

"So I have to… I have to marry him?"

"Unless you can convince them there is some other alternative," her father said. "I'm not sure what else can be done. You are beyond our reach. This is something we never wanted for you."

Fury filled her anew. "But you knew it could happen. You knew all along, and I didn't."

"We never wanted you to be afraid of your own shadow," her mother said.

"Well, I don't want to be afraid of my own shadow. But I should have been warned to be afraid of charming Spanish men who tried to talk me up on the street." She hung up, and as soon as she did the door swung open. And there was Felipe.

Immediately, she was filled with regret.

He crossed the room, taking the phone from her hand. Why had she hung up? Who knew how long it would be before she was able to speak to her parents again.

"I assume everything that I said would be confirmed was?" he asked.

"I assume you were listening in, based on your perfect timing."

He smiled. "You know me so well already. We're going to be the perfect married couple."

"I don't understand. Marry somebody else. Why does it have to be me?"

He reached out then, grabbing hold of her hand and tugging her up out of bed. She was still wearing nothing more than the hospital gown, and she felt a breeze at her backside. She gasped, realizing that there was nothing but a thin pair of white cotton panties separating her from being bare back there.

His golden eyes were blazing then, blazing with that kind of fire and intensity she had sensed was inside him. And more than that. Fire, and brimstone. She had the sudden sense that there was hell contained inside this man. And whether it was just the shock wearing off, or a sudden connection with the reality she found herself in, for the first time she was afraid of him. Really afraid.

She found herself being dragged over to a window. Heavy drapes obscured the view, and he flung them back, roughly maneuvering her so that she was facing the vista before them. A large, sprawling city, nothing overly modern. Villas with red clay roofs, churches with tall steeples and iron bells hanging in the towers. And beyond that, the mountains.

"Do you see this?" he asked. "This is my country. For decades it has been ruled by a madman. A madman more concerned by power—by shoring up all of the money, all of the means through which he could blackmail—than caring for the people that live down there. And in that time I have spent decades doing what I can do in order to change things once I assume the throne. Working toward having the military on my side. Toward earning as much money as I could personally to make a difference the minute I had control. I have been making contacts and arrangements behind the scenes so that the moment my father's body is put into the dirt a new dawn will rise on this country. I never wanted to take it by civil war.

No, not when the cost would be so dear in terms of life. At least, I didn't want to take it in an open civil war. But that is exactly what I have been fighting for years. Playing the part of debauched playboy while I maneuvered in the background. You are part of that plan. And I will be damned if I allow you to do anything to mess it up. There is no amount of compassion that could move me at this point, Princess. Nothing that will stir me to change my path. I will be the King of Santa Milagro. And you… You can be the queen. You can help fix all the evil that has befallen my people, and you can improve the lives of yours, as well. Or you can go back to life as a bored sorority girl in the city. I'm sure that's an existence, as well. And all of these people… Well, they can slide into the sea."

She had to smooth her fingers over her eyebrows to make sure they hadn't been singed off during that fiery tirade. "Am I really so important to your plans?"

"Everybody knew that you were supposed to marry my father. And the things he would have done to you… But if you marry me, and you do so willingly…it will mend the fences between Santa Milagro and Verloren. It will do much to fix the image of my country—and me—in the media. I need everything in my power. Absolutely everything. All the pieces that I have set out to collect. I will let nothing fall by the wayside. Including you."

"And if I don't?"

"I didn't think I could possibly make that more clear. If you don't there will be destruction. For everyone. Everyone you love. Everyone you will love."

She blinked. "Are you going to have people killed?"

"No. I'll only make them wish they were dead."

"And how will that help your *improve your image* attempt?" she asked with a boldness she didn't feel.

"I'm not so stupid that I would go about it in the public view. But your New York parents...they are vulnerable. And suitably low visibility. Nonetheless, I can ruin them financially. He works with American politicians. And believe me, if I offer the right incentives, I can decimate his patient base, his reputation. Because far better to have an alliance with a prince than continue to support a specific physician."

Ice settled in her stomach. She believed him. Believed he would do that. Harm her parents. And if she allowed that...what sort of daughter would she be? They had protected her all her life. The least she could do was protect them in kind.

He smiled, and something in that smile made it impossible for her to doubt him. And then his expression shifted, and he returned to being that charming-looking man she had seen on the street in New York. "Now, you can't possibly meet my people in that hospital gown. Rest for tonight. Tomorrow... Tomorrow we shall set about fashioning you into a queen."

Felipe walked into his father's room. It was dark, the curtains drawn, none of the lights on.

"Good evening, Father," he said, sweeping toward the bed.

"Your jacket is crooked," his father said by way of greeting.

Felipe lifted his arm, tugging his sleeves down, hating the reflex. "It is not," he returned. "And you're very nearly blind, so even if it was, there would be no way for you to tell."

It was a strange thing, seeing this man in this state. He had always been fearful to Felipe when he'd been a child. And now, here he was, drained, shrunken. And still, something twisted with something sour whenever he looked at him.

This man, who had abused and tortured him and his mother for years. A slap across her face when Felipe was "in disarray."

He could remember well his mother being hit so hard it left an instant bruise beneath her eye. And then her makeup artist had been charged with making it invisible before they went to present themselves in the ballroom as the perfect royal family.

A facade of perfection. Something his father excelled at. He had convinced his country of the perfection of his family and the perfection of his rule. The citizens of Santa Milagro slowly and effectively stripped of their freedom. Of art, education and hope.

All things Felipe would see restored. Though he would never be able to fix what had become of his mother, at least he could restore Santa Milagro itself.

There had always been the temptation to try and claim the country by force, but that would only entail more loss of life.

There was enough blood shed already. Blood that felt as if it stained his hands.

"Is that any way to talk to your dying father?"

"Probably not. But since when have I cared? I only wanted you to know something."

"What is that?"

"I found her. The princess."

His father stirred. "My princess?"

A smile curved Felipe's lips. "No. She's mine now. I'm

going to make her my wife. There is nothing you can do about it. Not from your deathbed."

"You're a bastard," his father said, his voice thin, reedy and as full of venom as it had ever been. But he had no power now.

"Don't I wish that were true," Felipe said, twisting his voice into the cruelest version of itself he could manage. Projecting the sort of cruelty that he had learned from the man lying before him. "If only I were a bastard, rather than your flesh and blood. You have no idea how much I would pay to make that so."

"The feeling," his father said, the words broken by a ragged cough, "is mutual." He wiped a shaking hand over his brow. "I never was able to break you."

"Not for lack of trying," Felipe said. "But I do hope that I will go down in history as one of your greatest failures. The only truly sad thing is that you will not be here to see it."

He turned to leave his father's room. Then paused. "However, if you're still alive by the time the wedding rolls around I will be sure to send you an invitation. I'll understand that you won't be feeling up to attending."

He continued out of his father's room then, striding down the hall and on to the opposite wing of the palace where his rooms were. It was only then that he acknowledged the slight tremor in his own hand.

He flung open the doors to his chamber, crossing the length of the space, and took a large bottle of whiskey from the bar that was installed at the back wall. He looked at the glass that he kept positioned there—always, for easy access—and decided it was not needed. He took the cap off the bottle and lifted it to his lips, tilting it back and trying to focus on the burn as the alcohol slid down his throat.

It took so much more for him to feel it now. So much more for him to feel anything.

He slammed the bottle back down onto the bar. And he waited. Waited for something to make that feeling of being tainted go away. It was because he had gone into his father's room. Or maybe it was because of the princess who resided down the hall against her will.

Or maybe it was just because his father's blood ran through his veins.

Felipe roared, turning toward the wall and striking it with his forearm, his fist closed. He repeated the motion. Over and over and over again as pain shot up to his shoulder, and all the way down to his tightly closed fingers.

Then he lowered his arm, shaking it out. He took a deep breath, the silence in the room settling over him. He looked down, and he noticed a trail of blood leaking out from beneath his now crooked shirtsleeves.

He frowned. Then reached down and grabbed hold of the fabric, straightening his cuffs. And took another drink.

When Briar awoke the next morning she was greeted by three stylists. A man dressed in a shocking green coat, wielding a pair of golden scissors. A woman in a skin-tight fuchsia dress, and another wearing a pale blue top and a navy-colored skirt.

"The prince has ordered that we help prepare you for your public debut," the woman in pink said, her features seeming to grow sharper as she examined Briar.

"I don't normally wear hospital gowns," she said, her

voice stiff. "But I kind of left home without a chance to gather any of my clothes."

The woman waved a hand, the shocking neon finger-nails a blur against her brown skin. "None of them would have been acceptable anyway. I'm confident in that fact."

After that, she found herself being plucked from bed and herded into the bathroom where she was instructed to get into the shower, where she would find acceptable soaps. She bristled at the idea that somehow what she had used before wasn't acceptable, but gladly walked into the massive tiled facility and stood beneath the hot spray for longer than was strictly necessary.

Then she began to scrub her skin with the toiletries provided and had to concede the fact that it was essentially like cleansing herself with silk. Perhaps, she also had to concede that as nice as the items in her childhood home were, they weren't palace material.

Then she got defensive again when she was seated in front of a vanity and that man with the golden scissors began to paw at her hair.

"Don't cut too much off," she all but snarled.

"I'm sorry," he said, "where did you go to school for hair?"

"I didn't. But it's grown out of my head for the past twenty-two years, so I have to say I'm pretty well educated on that situation."

He appraised her reflection in the mirror, squinting his eyes. "No. Not more than I am. You should not have straight hair."

"Well, clearly I disagree with you," she said, feeling defensive.

"Your bone structure agrees with me."

There was no argument after that. And she had to

admit that when he was finished she appreciated the curls in her hair in a way she didn't normally. He had managed to find a nice middle ground between the tightly wound natural curl and the board-straight style she normally aimed for. The fact that she didn't hate it was a little bit annoying.

She had a similar interaction with the stylist who was intent on choosing silhouettes that Briar normally avoided. She was averse to things that clung too tightly to her curves, but the woman in bright pink seemed to think that Briar needed to show off a bit more.

The makeup artist didn't believe in subtlety, either, and by the end of it Briar barely recognized the woman in the mirror. Or rather, she almost did. Because the tall, slim creature with her eye-catching curls and slim figure wrapped tightly in a blaze-orange dress, bright pink blush on her cheeks and gold on her lips, looked more like Queen Amaani than she did herself.

It was becoming more and more difficult to deny the reality of the situation.

Although, resemblance didn't confirm genetics, but her parents had told her it was true. And even if they hadn't…it would be very difficult to push it aside now.

"Beautiful," the man in green said.

She felt complimented, but at the same time didn't really want the compliment as she was being made beautiful for a man she didn't really want to feel beautiful for.

She said nothing, but her beauty team didn't seem to care. Instead, they packed up their things and left as quickly and efficiently as they had arrived.

Briar wobbled on the high heels she was wearing then sat quickly on the edge of the bed. She put her hand to her chest and looked at the mirror that hung across the room, looked at the wide-eyed, undeniably beautiful woman staring back at her.

She was a princess. Really and truly. And she was supposed to marry a prince who was quite possibly the maddest bastard on the planet.

The door to her room opened again and a man she hadn't seen before appeared. "His Majesty would appreciate it if you would join him for breakfast. Provided you are dressed suitably."

"Does that mean he didn't want me to show up in a hospital gown?"

The servant didn't react, his expression carefully blank. "He did not specify."

"Well, I imagine I'm suitable." She stood, following him out of her bedroom. She had been tempted, if only for a moment, to deem herself unsuitable and stay in her bedroom. But she had been in there for two days and eventually she was going to have to face her adversary. Face the man who claimed he was going to marry her whether she wanted him to or not.

And she was going to have to try to get out of it.

She walked silently with the servant, the only sound in the corridor the clicking of her high heels on the flag-stone. The man opened the door to what she presumed was the dining room and stood to the side. "This way."

He didn't enter with her. Instead, she heard the doors close firmly behind her and found herself standing alone in a cavernous room with Prince Felipe. He was seated at the opposite end of the table from her, a newspaper to his left, a cup of coffee to his right.

"Good morning," he said.

Then, from behind the paper, he produced a velvet

ring box. He set it firmly in front of him then said nothing more about it. "Have a seat," he said.

"As you wish," she returned, taking her seat in the farthest possible place from him, nearest the door.

"That is not what I meant," he said.

"But it is what you said."

He chuckled and folded the paper then retrieved the ring box and picked up his cup. He stood then, and she was reminded of how tall he was. How imposing. He walked across the room and sat down next to her. If he was fazed at all, he didn't show it.

"You seem to have woken up in a good mood, Briar."

"That's the first time you've called me that," she said. "Apart from when you were pretending to be José."

"I suppose it doesn't benefit me to be at odds with you," he said, tilting his head to the side, a dent appearing between his brows. As though he was truly considering this for the first time. "If you are more comfortable being called Briar in conversation, then I will call you that. However, in public I will refer to you by your given name."

"A given name I don't remember being given."

"Do any of us really remember being given our names? I know I certainly don't." He placed his index finger firmly against the top of the ring box and slid it toward her. "See if this is to your satisfaction."

"It won't be," she said, not making any move toward the box.

"I doubt that. The diamond is practically large enough to eradicate world hunger."

"Then eradicate world hunger. Don't put it on my finger."

"I will make a donation to charity that matches the value. Put it on your finger."

"No," she responded. "I have been given no real compelling reason why I have to actually marry you. It's only because you're choosing to consider me payment for a debt, which I think we can both agree is a bit archaic. You say that your father is a monster, so I don't understand why you want to be monstrous, as well."

"Because I will be a better monster," he said. "Anyway, I have explained my terms, and they will not change."

"Well I don't—"

"Do you want to meet your parents? King Behrendt and Queen Amaani?"

A strange, yawning void opened up inside her chest. One that she hadn't realized was there until that moment. And she flashed back to earlier when she had seen her reflection in the mirror and realized how much she favored the queen. Realized that there was most certainly truth in the stories she had been told about her lineage.

She loved the mother and father she knew, and nothing could ever replace them. But she had other parents. Parents who hadn't actually wanted to give her up. Parents who had done it for her protection.

A king and queen who had lived halfway across the world from her for almost her entire life. A king and queen that she could meet.

That longing was an ache, so acute, so intense, that it stole her breath.

But she refused to respond to him. Apparently, she didn't need to, because only a moment later it became clear that her longing must have been written across her features.

"Excellent," he said. "If you ever want to meet your

parents, if you want to see the palace again… We can always attend the annual ball they throw every year in October. I hear you loved it when you were a little girl. There is always spiced cider, which I'm told was your favorite."

It hit her in the chest with the force of a brick. That feeling. That nostalgia. That hook she felt in her gut whenever the air began to chill and the leaves started to fall.

It was what she remembered. Oh, she didn't remember it in pictures. Didn't remember it as an actual event. But it lived somewhere inside her. Resided in her bones. It transcended specific moments and images and existed in the realm of feeling. Deep and powerful. It was a root; she couldn't deny it. It always had been. A part of her that connected her to the earth, that ran beneath the surface of all that she was. That had formed her into who she was now.

She wanted to see it. She wanted to connect that with something real. With something more than a feeling.

"You remember," he said, the amusement in his voice almost enraging. "And you do want it. More than anything. You have very expressive eyes, *querida*. All the better for me."

All the better for him to manipulate her, he meant. And he was doing it. Doing it with all the skill of a master. She suddenly felt like a puppet whose strings had been cut. Like someone who had been restrained all her life, who was left standing there with an endless array of choice.

Her parents weren't here. She didn't like Felipe, and he needed her. Which meant she was under no pressure at all to behave a certain way. As long as she was here, she was doing his bidding and he couldn't—and wouldn't—

lash out at her so long as she didn't bring her behavior into the public eye.

She didn't have to behave. She didn't have to do anything for anyone.

She didn't have to be perfect.

"Of course I want to meet my parents," she said, not bothering to soften her tone. "Who wouldn't want to understand where they came from?"

"It will be impossible for you to meet your family, of course, should you fail them in the way that you are suggesting you might."

"They sent me across the world, pretended I was dead, in order to avoid this fate for me."

"No, they wished for you to avoid my father. However, a marriage of convenience is not uncommon between royals. And I am not my father. Believe me. It matters. That is not just an incidental. Had the marriage been set between you and I from the moment you were born…they would have happily handed you over. What I can offer them, what I can offer your country, and what yours can offer mine, is no small thing. Conversely, what I can do if you disappoint me on this score is no small thing. Do you honestly think that your mother and father would be content to allow you to marry a doctor on the Upper East Side?"

"They sent me to be raised by one. I'm not entirely certain why one wouldn't be good enough for me to marry."

"But you were never intended to live there forever. You were always meant to come back and assume your place. Tell me… What did you expect to do with your life?"

"I was an art major."

He made a dismissive sound. "So you're poised to become an incredibly useful member of society. I'm terribly sad to have interrupted that trajectory."

Anger fired through her veins, and since she wasn't worried about making friends with him, she let it show. "Art is important."

"Of course. It's the thing that people worry about after all of their necessities are met."

"It's one of the things that makes the world beautiful. It gives people hope. It's part of moving from surviving to living."

A smile curved his lips. "I seem to have found a bit of passion in you. That is encouraging. I would put you in charge of the art program. For all the schools in my country. You will have the opportunity to change the face of education in this country. My father has kept things quite austere, it may not surprise you to learn. When I say he has been something of an evil dictator I am not exaggerating. That is not the kind of job offer you're going to get in Manhattan. What else are you going to do with that degree? You going to marry someone successful and plan all his parties for him? I grant you that often princesses can be quite decorative, but my queen will not be. I will use you in whatever capacity you see fit, whatever way you can find to improve my country."

He spoke with…well, sincerity, which was the most surprising thing. That he seemed to so easily hand this to her. The chance to reconnect with her parents, with her heritage, and the chance to make a difference. All by using the subject that she was most passionate about.

"And you should see the art collection we have in the palace. Just sitting in the basement waiting to be curated. Our museums need to be opened. We have been in the dark ages. It is time that we come into the light. And if—as you say—art is a part of living and not surviving, then help my people live."

It was strange, because she could actually see that he cared about this. About his country. That of all the things in the entire world, this might be the only thing that mattered to him. She might be at a disadvantage here, but so was he. Because he cared about this. And he needed her. Needed her to cooperate. Needed her to help insulate his image.

"And if I get up in front of the entire world when you try to announce our engagement and tell them that you kidnapped me?" She had to ask.

"If I go down, Princess, we are going down in flames together. I promise you that. I'm not a man to make idle threats. I have been lying in wait for years, waiting for the moment when I might liberate my kingdom, when I might save my people. Believe me when I tell you I will not be stopped now. I would not say that I am a man consumed with serving the greater good. I don't really care about whether it's good or not. I care about serving my goal. My goal is to make this country great. My goal is to liberate the people in it. Whatever I have to do."

He slid the ring closer to her again. "Now. Put it on."

She hesitated for a moment before reaching out and curling her fingers around the box. Then she opened it slowly. Her breath caught in her throat. It truly was beautiful. A stunning diamond set into an ornate platinum setting. Definitely designed to tempt a woman on the fence about accepting a marriage proposal.

If it was a show of love it would be personal.

It hit her then, with the speed and impact of a freight

train, what it would mean to marry him. It would mean never having a real boyfriend. It would mean never falling in love. And it would mean…

She looked up at him, her heart slamming against her breastbone. Images flashed through her mind. Him touching her. Kissing her. She had never kissed a man before, unless you counted that time he had kissed her when she was unconscious. And she didn't really. Except, it was difficult not to. Because it had most certainly been the first time another person's lips had touched hers. And thinking of it now made them burn.

"Did you have questions?" he asked.

"I don't have another choice. Do I?"

"We always have choices. It's just that the results of those choices are going to be better or worse. You have one choice that doesn't ruin a great many lives. That isn't having no choices."

"One requires me to be completely selfish, though." And if she decided to walk away from him, she supposed that she could go back to life as she had always known it. She would simply ruin an entire nation that she hadn't known much about until this week. Would never meet her parents. But she could go back to how things were. Could pretend that none of this had happened.

"And if I were you, that is perhaps the choice I would make."

His dark eyes glittered, and she had a feeling that his comment had been calculated. Because the moment he had said that, she had known that her decision was made. She wasn't him. She wasn't, and she never would be. Her parents had always instilled in her the fact that having money as they did didn't make her better, didn't make them better. That she had been given a great many advantages and was responsible for making the best of those advantages.

She had been intent on doing that. As soon as she had finished school she had planned on getting involved in inner-city art programs, in establishing funds and foundations. She was being given the opportunity to do that here. And more.

The influence she would have as a queen was inestimable.

She wrapped her hand around the ring box. "Okay. I'll do it."

He didn't smile. Didn't gloat. No, he reacted in a completely different way to what she had imagined he might do. His handsome face set an expression of grim determination. "Good. And it is done. The announcement will be made tomorrow. And we are going to have a ball celebrating our engagement. I have already sent out invitations."

"Ahead of my acceptance?"

"I never doubted you."

The words hit her strangely, bounced around inside her chest, ricocheting off her heart. They made her angry, but they made her feel something else, too. Something she couldn't quite put a finger on. Something she didn't want to put a finger—or anything else—on.

"Perhaps you should. Someday I might surprise you."

He shook his head. "Good people are rarely surprising, Briar. It's bad people you have to watch out for." He stood then. "You should order yourself a coffee." He turned to walk out of the room.

"Are you a bad person?"

His expression turned grave, deadly serious, which

was strange. "I am… Whatever I am, I am beyond help. If I were you, I wouldn't try."

Then he left, leaving her alone with her fear, her doubt and a diamond.

CHAPTER FIVE

IT WAS THE headline the next morning. That Prince Felipe Carrión de la Viña Cortez was engaged to the long-lost Princess of Verloren. He assumed it was not the best way for the king and queen to discover that he had found their daughter, but he was going to send them an invitation to the engagement party so they could hardly be too upset.

Though he didn't think they would come. No, they would assume that it was some kind of trap, of course. It would take time. It would take time for anybody to trust that he wasn't as conniving as his father.

Starting with the kidnapping of a princess was perhaps not the best opening move, all things considered. But that was one thing that he and Briar were going to have to discuss.

He flung the doors to her bedchamber open, unfazed by the gasp and eruption of movement that resulted. He saw nothing but a flash of curl and a blur of brown skin as she dashed behind a changing screen.

"I'm not dressed!"

"And I'm your fiancé," he said. "Which is exactly what I came to speak to you about. You cannot behave this way in my presence. I cannot have the world thinking that I forced you into this."

She poked her head out from the side of the divider. "But you did."

"Sure. But we're not going to advertise that, are we? It undermines my aim for building bridges between nations."

"Well, God forbid you could build an actual bridge," she said, disappearing behind the divider again. He heard the rustle of clothes.

"Don't dress on my account."

She made an exasperated sound then appeared a moment later wearing a black pencil skirt and a bright green crop top. She was stunning. She had been from the beginning, but the new wardrobe, the makeover, provided to her by his staff, had truly brought out the uncommonness of her beauty. It had elevated her from mere beauty to someone who would turn heads everywhere she went.

Exactly what he wanted in a queen.

He enjoyed her ability to stand up to him, as well. Had she no spine at all he would have kept her, certainly, but it would have been a much greater trial. It would have made him think too much of his mother.

And he knew where that ended.

"I'm not going to stand in front of you in my underwear."

"You will eventually."

She paled slightly. "Well. We'll cross that bridge when we come to it."

"The bridge you just accused me of not building?"

"It's a different bridge, obviously."

"Just clarifying. I wish to give you a tour of the castle."

She looked startled by that. "Why?"

"Because you live here. And you will live here for the foreseeable future. Don't you want a tour of your home?"

"I guess it's practical. But I don't know why you're giving it to me."

"I am going to be your husband. And we are going to be required to make a great many public appearances together. You will have to learn to act as though my presence doesn't disgust you."

"I was never a very good liar," she said, looking at him with those fathomless dark eyes, her expression almost comically serene.

"Well, get better at it." He extended his arm. "Shall we?"

She accepted the offered arm slowly, curving her fingers around him as though she thought he was a poisonous serpent. Something about that light, tentative touch sent a shock of heat through his body.

That electricity that had been there from the moment he had seen her pulsed through him with renewed strength. She had been quite pitiful after her accident, and that—along with the logistics of convincing her to marry him—had pushed some of that attraction onto the back burner. But he was reminded now. With ferocity. He was also reminded that it had been a very long time since he'd had a woman in his bed. He had been too focused on getting all the pieces in play to see to the typical pleasures he filled his time with.

"You've seen the dining room already," he said, indicating the room to their left. "My chambers are that way. My father is kept in another wing entirely, and you have no reason to ever set foot in that part of the palace." The old man might be incapacitated, but he still didn't want Briar anywhere near his father.

The shock of protectiveness that slammed into his chest surprised him. Briar—as far as he was concerned—

was a means to an end. He did not have particularly strong feelings about her. But he did have particularly strong feelings about his father and the sort of influence he wielded over women. He didn't want that old man to put one drop of poison into Briar's ear. Not when he knew full well that it was the sort of poison that could be fatal.

"I don't think I want to, all things considered." She hesitated for a moment. "He's really dying?"

"Any day now, truly. His body has been failing him for quite some time. There is no hope left. Nothing to be done. Just waiting for him to choke on his spite and bile."

"You don't sound…sad at all."

"I'm not. I thought I had made that perfectly clear. I hate my father. I'm not simply ambivalent toward him. I loathe him. My legacy shall be upending his."

She said nothing to that, though she shifted to the side of him, the soft swell of her breast brushing up against his biceps. A simple touch, one that would have barely registered had it been any other woman. At any other moment. But he was going to marry this woman.

For the first time, that part of the plan truly settled in his mind. She would be the mother of his children. And he would need her to be…happy. That had not been part of the plan when he had first conceived it. He had not considered her happiness—her feelings of any sort—when he had decided that he needed to bring her here and make her his. Why would he? Considering that would run counter to his objective. He didn't like anything getting in the way of his objective.

And considering it now had nothing to do with the goodness of his heart. If he possessed a heart he very much doubted it had any goodness in it. But she would give birth to his children, and she would need to be there for them. He knew too well the alternative.

Suddenly, the promise of art programs was much more than simple bribery. "I meant what I said," he said. "About the art collection. About the programs. You will be in charge of those. You can appoint an entire team to help you with teaching, with organization. I will give you a very generous budget. The country has fallen on difficult financial times under my father's rule, but I have made billions on my own. And I have kept it all out of the country, tightly under my control so my father couldn't get his hands on any of it. But that will change once he's gone."

She stopped walking, looking at him, her expression full of confusion. "Why are you giving me this? It's for your country, right? It isn't for me."

"My aim is not for you to be miserable."

"Why do you care?"

"Because I know what it's like to exist beneath the rule of a totalitarian regime. My father was a dictator to the country, but he was even worse to those who lived under his roof. It will not be so, not in my house. I will not subject my wife or my children to such things."

Her mouth dropped open. "Children."

"Of course we will have children. The single most important act for a ruler is to produce an heir, is it not?"

"I...I suppose. I hadn't really thought about it."

"Of course you haven't. You were raised as a commoner. But it is a requirement. I have to carry on my line."

She frowned. "But I... But we..."

"Do you not want children?"

She frowned. "I...I do. I... Things are different now,

because I'm going to meet my parents. My biological parents. But I always wanted someone in my life that I shared a genetic bond with. Which is silly. It doesn't matter. Blood doesn't matter. All that matters is that somebody loves you. And my parents—the ones that raised me—they love me. But still."

"You don't have to explain yourself to me," he said. "I'm a man entirely driven by the need for vengeance. I'm hardly going to call your motives into question."

"Yes, I want children. But I didn't anticipate having them… Now. Or with…" She was blushing. Her cheeks turning a dusky rose.

"With me?" He finished for her.

"Well. Yes. You're a stranger."

"I won't be. By that point." They wandered down the long hall, and all the way to a pair of blue, gilded double doors that were firmly closed. "This is where we will hold the ball where we celebrate our upcoming nuptials." He flung them open then reached out for her this time. "Come with me, Princess."

She took his hand reluctantly, but eventually curved her delicate fingers around his. He smiled. He knew full well how to put people at ease, but he hadn't done the best job with her since that first day. Since that first moment.

He would do well to charm her. She would certainly be happier. And he knew how to charm women. He had been told a great many times that he was very good at it. And, if the notches on his bedpost were any indicator, it was the truth. It would not cost him to turn on that part of himself for this woman.

Now that he had her, now the she had agreed…

"Do you know how to dance?"

She laughed. "Of course I do. I had an entire…coming out."

"A debutante?"

"Yes."

"You really are excellent. And your parents did a wonderful job raising you. Because they knew that this would ultimately be where you'd land."

She frowned. "Well. If what you say is true, then they hoped I would end up back in my country and not in yours at all."

"Perhaps." He shifted their positions, keeping hold of her hand, then he wrapped his arm around her waist and pulled her up against him. "Would you care to practice?"

Her dark eyes widened, her full lips falling open. "I don't need to practice."

"The world will be watching when we take our first dance as a couple. It is not enough to simply know how to dance. You have to know how to move with me." And with that, with no music playing and no sound in the room but their feet moving over the glossy marble, he swept her into the first step of a waltz.

She followed beautifully, her movements graceful, but her expression spoke far too readily of her feelings.

He leaned in slightly. "You must work at looking as though my touch doesn't disgust you."

As he spoke the words, he realized that he must work at making sure his touch didn't disgust her. Yes, the relationship had started with force, but there was no reason it could not be mutually satisfying. Oh, there would never be any love, nothing like that. He didn't believe in the emotion. Even if he did, he wasn't capable of feeling it. But they could have a reasonable amount of companionship.

They could certainly have more than violence and death. Than aching loss. Yes, they could have more than that.

He moved his hand slowly down the curve of her waist, settling it more firmly on her hip. She looked up at him, her dark gaze meeting his, the confusion there evident. He knew why she was confused. She didn't find his touch repellent at all. And she couldn't figure out why.

"Don't feel bad," he said, keeping his voice soft. "I'm very experienced at this. I promise you I could take you from shouting at me in anger to screaming my name in pleasure in only a few moments."

Color suffused her cheeks and she tried to pull away from him. He held her firmly. Didn't let her leave. Kept on dancing. "You're ashamed of that. Of the fact that you enjoy me touching you." He was fascinated by that. That somebody would waste one moment being ashamed of something that brought them pleasure. He'd had very little of it in his childhood, and he could admit that he had possibly gone overboard with it once he had gotten out from beneath his father's roof. Once he had discovered women. Once he had discovered that, as profoundly terrible as his father could make him feel, a woman's hands on his skin, a soft touch, could make him feel that much better.

But whether or not it had been too much, he didn't regret it. No. He never let himself regret feeling good.

"I don't understand," she said, her voice flat, not bothering to deny the accusation.

"There's very little to understand with chemistry, *querida*. And there is very little point in fighting ours. We are to be married, after all." Her flush deepened and she looked away from him. "Did you imagine that you would be a martyr in my bed? I promise you, you could start out as serene and filled with sacrifices as Joan of Arc, but in the end, when I made you burn, it would not be in the way you're thinking."

"You're so arrogant," she said, her voice vibrating with some strong emotion he couldn't place. "Assuming that I'm not comfortable with this because I feel shame. It didn't occur to you that maybe—just maybe—I'm not feeling exactly what you think?"

"Sorry," he said, knowing he didn't sound apologetic in the least. "But you're a little too late in your denial. And even if your words haven't already betrayed you, your body betrays you, Princess. Your eyes…" He lifted his hand, tracing a line just beneath her left eye. "They've gotten darker looking at me, your pupils expanding. This speaks of arousal, did you know?"

She swallowed visibly. "My eyes are dark. I sincerely doubt you noticed anything of the kind."

"All right. Then let's move on. There is color in your cheeks. You're blushing."

"Perhaps I'm angry. Maybe that's why."

"I suspect you're angry, as well. More at yourself than at me." He moved his thumb down the curve of her cheek, to her lower lip, sliding it slowly over that soft, lush skin. "You're trembling here. And your breathing… It has grown very shallow. Quick."

"And that," she said, her voice unsteady now, "could be fear."

"Yes. But you don't strike me as the kind of woman who scares easily."

"I don't suppose being hit by a taxi and kidnapped, then taken half a world away, scaring me, would qualify as *scaring easily.*"

He laughed. "No. I don't suppose it would. Still…" He moved his thumb even slower across her lower lip. "I don't think you're afraid of me. I think you're afraid of what you might do." He moved in slowly and she sucked in a sharp breath, drawing backward. "Yes. You're afraid of what you might want. That's the scary thing, isn't it? Knowing that I'm not Prince Charming. Knowing that I am the monster. And wanting me anyway. That does make you unique. Most women only know the surface. Most of them have not had the pleasure of being kidnapped by me. They want the facade. You know what's underneath and you want me still. I wonder…"

A strange sense of disquiet filled his chest and he did his best to ignore it. He couldn't afford to be growing a conscience now. Couldn't afford to be concerned with her or her feelings. He needed to seduce her. She was supposed to be his wife, after all. He was hardly going to live in a sexless marriage. Then again, he wasn't entirely sure he was going to remain faithful during the course of their marriage. That would depend. On a great many factors. Namely what would keep the peace in the palace. It was entirely possible that she would not want all of his attentions focused on her.

But as he had realized only a few minutes ago, her happiness was going to have to come into consideration. Something new, and strange. Needing to care about the emotions of another person. If only to keep her from… Well. He had no desire to repeat the sins of his father. That was as far as he would go with that line of thinking today.

"What do you wonder?" she asked. It was strange that she seemed to be asking the question genuinely. That she did not seem to be teasing or testing him. He had a very limited amount of experience with people who were genuine in any fashion. But Briar seemed genuine. She was sharp, and she possessed a rather whip-smart wit. But even so, there was something…well, something untested about her. Young. Innocent. In his circle, in his world, there were very few innocent people. Everyone was guilty of something.

He supposed eventually he would find out what she was guilty of. Because there was no way she was everything she seemed on the surface. Nobody was.

Still. The way she asked the question…

"I wonder if it would be the same for anyone," he said, his voice hard. "Perhaps you're not unique. Perhaps any woman, faced with the possibility of marrying a prince who was set to become a king, given the chance to be a queen, would overlook the fact that I'm a bit…beastly."

"I'm not looking anything over," she pointed out. "You're holding quite a few things hostage—including me—in order to get me to agree to the marriage."

He found himself oddly relieved by that, and he didn't know why. "That is true."

He was still touching her lower lip, and the color in her cheeks was only growing more intense. "You can stop that now," she said.

"I'm not sure that I want to."

"Well, I want you to."

He dropped his hand down to his side. And he was gratified when she let out a long, slow breath that he was certain spoke of disappointment. She wished that he would push harder. She did. Whether she admitted it or not, she did.

"It must be nice," he said, releasing his hold on her

and stepping back from her. "Releasing all responsibility in a situation."

"What are you talking about?"

"I'm a kidnapper. A kidnapper, a blackmailer… Well, it's not a long list, but it is a fairly damning one. You, on the other hand… What are you? Victimized, I suppose. You have no other option but to marry me. And certainly, it benefits you in a great many ways, but you're able to claim that you're not actually swayed by the title, by the money…when in fact, you might be."

"Stop it," she said. "You're twisting the situation. It's bad enough without you adding gaslight."

He drew back, feeling as though she had slapped him. He *was* manipulating the situation, and he found that it was something of an impulse on his end. Which ran counter to the fact that he had just realized he needed to do something to make her happy. But he didn't know how to…have a real conversation. He didn't know how to do anything other than poke and prod, and attempt to make himself come out with the advantage.

He didn't know how to connect.

She seemed to. She had asked a question. And it had been genuine. Part of his answer had been, as well.

"Very well," he said, moving away from her. "We can finish for the day."

"What else am I supposed to do with my time?"

"Anything you like. Except for returning to New York. But I have informed my staff of the position that you will be filling after our marriage, and it's possible that you can begin organizing the art collection right away."

She looked shocked. "I can?"

He waved a hand. "Yes. Why would I prevent you

from doing that? It was one of the things I used to bribe you with."

She blinked. "I suppose so."

"I don't want you to be miserable. Sure, the foundation for the marriage might be kidnapping and blackmail, but I don't see why you can't enjoy yourself."

"You know I think that might be the most honest thing you said since we met."

"What?"

"That you don't understand why I can't enjoy myself even though I've been blackmailed and kidnapped."

"The situation is what it is. Make of it what you will. I suppose I will see you again for our engagement party."

She looked relieved. Relieved that she wouldn't be seeing him for a while. Well, that was going to have to pass. But there was time.

He turned and walked away from his fiancée, the woman who was wearing his ring, who didn't even want to be in the same room with him. And he ignored the tightening in his gut and below his belt as he did. She was beautiful, but she wasn't special.

No woman was. No one person was. He wasn't sentimental; he didn't believe in that sort of thing.

But as he walked down the corridor toward his office he had to make a concerted effort to banish the image in his mind of that wide-eyed, genuine look that had been written on her face when she had asked him what he wondered. With nothing but curiosity. Nothing but honesty.

And as he sat down at his desk he did his best to banish the grim thought that her honesty wouldn't last long. Not with him. That kind of openness, the little bit of innocence that she possessed, would be snuffed out by the darkness inside him.

It was as inevitable as her becoming his queen. And as necessary, as well.

There was nothing that could be done. And he would waste no time feeling guilty about it.

Guilt was for men who could afford to have consciences. He was not one of those men.

CHAPTER SIX

THE ENGAGEMENT PARTY came more quickly than Briar was prepared for. The moment when Felipe was going to present her for the entire world to see as his fiancée. Yes, the world at large knew, but this was different. This was the first time she was actually going to make an appearance. The first time she was going to have to contend with it.

She had been presented with two couture gowns to try on for the event. And her stylists were currently in a heated debate as to whether or not she should choose the pink or the blue.

Both were cut dramatically, designed to show off her figure, and billowed around her feet. Ultimately, she went with the blue. Because when she twirled, it moved effortlessly with her body. That, and it had a little bit more give around the hips. She had a feeling that she was going to need it. She was naturally thin, much to the chagrin of most of her friends at university, but even she felt a little bit constrained by a gown after a long evening of standing around eating. And the delicacies here at the palace really were amazing.

She supposed if one had to get kidnapped, getting kidnapped by a prince really was the way to go. Good food, good lodgings. And really amazing clothes.

As she was zipped into the beautiful blue gown, she looked down at the ring sparkling on her left hand. Right. There was that. The fact that her particular kidnapping had come with a fiancé. But also with a royal title. Of course, she supposed she had that title on her own.

Her stomach lurched a little bit when she remembered that her parents—her birth parents—had been invited to tonight's event. Would they come? Would this be the first night she saw them since she was a little girl? And what would she do? She had a feeling that she would crumble. Break down completely, which she hadn't done once since she had been kidnapped from her home in New York. That was strange, she realized then. That she hadn't cried yet.

She supposed part of it came down to the fact that she was afraid if she shed even one tear she would shed endless tears, and then they might never stop.

She sucked in a deep, shuddering breath and looked at her reflection. At the woman staring back at her who was less a stranger now than she had been a week ago. With the expertly applied makeup and the beautifully styled curls.

Panic fluttered in her breast, and she had to look away.

This wasn't the time to have a meltdown. She was going to have to save it for later. She would pencil it into her brand-new schedule. A gift from Prince Felipe. At least, she had been told. True to his word, she hadn't seen him between that moment in the ballroom and today.

There was a very large part of herself that was grateful for that. What had happened was…confusing. The fact that he had made her feel things. The kinds of things she had felt that first moment when she had seen him standing there on the street.

And she kept turning over what he had said to her. About what it meant that she liked him even knowing he was a monster. Well, like maybe wasn't the word for it. That she was attracted to him.

That she *wanted* him.

She turned away from her reflection, pressing her hand against her stomach.

"You will be fine, Princess," the stylist said, reading her nerves incorrectly. That was fine. She didn't care if he thought she was nervous about going to the ball. Well, she was. But it had to do with her parents. And it had to do with him. The man that she should be disgusted by. The man that she should hate.

The man that made her feel things no other man ever had.

She was herded down the hall, to an antechamber that was seemingly outside a private entrance to the ballroom. She knew that guests had already arrived. She also knew that she was going to be presented, along with the prince, in a formal way.

She understood all of that. She hadn't grown up as traditional royalty, but growing up as she had, with her father occupying a very prominent position in high places, she had been American royalty in some regards.

Ceremony was part of that upbringing. She supposed that was helpful. Of all the things that she did have to worry about at least she didn't have to learn this entirely new language of formality.

She didn't know what she expected. Didn't know who she had expected to guide her into the ballroom. But she hadn't expected Felipe. Or maybe she had, and there was simply no way for her to prepare herself for the sight of him.

He was… Well, it simply wasn't fair how good he looked in a suit. He really should look monstrous. Because she knew that he was one. That he was selfish. That he was willing to do anything to meet his ends, no matter who he heard. It didn't matter. It didn't diminish the intensity of his masculine beauty.

The perfection of those broad shoulders, the exquisitely sculpted face that was a work of art all on its own.

"You look beautiful," he said as though he had pulled the word she was thinking right out of her head. Except, she had been thinking that he was beautiful. And she would rather die than confess that. Still, she had a feeling that he knew. It seemed evident in the glint in those dark eyes, in the slight quirk of his full mouth.

He certainly wasn't a man who possessed humility. Why was that appealing? Why was anything about him appealing?

You're going to marry him. You're going to marry him and sleep with him.

Her entire body went hot. She shouldn't be thinking about this. Not now.

Really, she was going to have to put off thinking about it for as long as possible. And then when she did, she was going to have to wait until she was alone. Until he wasn't standing right in front of her acting like a visual reference for what was going to happen. So that she wasn't tempted to imagine what he might look like without those layers of fabric over that masculine physique.

She should be appalled by him. If there was any justice, if there was any logic involved in hormones, she should be appalled.

She had always thought herself above this kind of

ridiculousness. Apparently, she had just been waiting for the right kind of wrong man to get hot and bothered over.

"Are my parents in there?" That was the one thing she had to know.

"You're welcome," he said, his tone dry. And it took her a moment to remember that he had just called her beautiful. Well, she wasn't going to thank him for that. Mostly because she wanted to keep her interactions with him anything but cordial. For now. She supposed, since she had agreed to marry the man, she had to relax that eventually.

Maybe around the time that she let herself think about being intimate with him.

Maybe.

"Are they in there or not?"

"They are," he said. "And they have requested a private audience with you, which I will grant them after we've been formally introduced."

Suddenly, she felt dizzy, but rather than reaching out to steady herself against the wall, she found herself pitching forward. She stretched her hand out, her fingertips coming into contact with his chest. Then she swayed. And he caught her around the waist, pulling her up against his body. "Are you okay?"

She looked up at him, or rather, at his Adam's apple, at the sharp line of his jaw, and then the wicked curve of his lips. She could feel his heart raging beneath her palm. And she wondered if his heart always beat so hard, if it always beat so fast. "No," she said, her tone hushed. "How can I be okay? I always knew that I was adopted. I always knew that I had birth parents out there somewhere. But I never expected to meet them. I certainly didn't expect them to be a king and queen. And I didn't expect them to have given me up reluctantly. To have given me up to protect me."

She found herself blinking back tears and wondering if her mascara was waterproof.

And he looked... Well, for the first time since she had met him Felipe looked afraid. As if her tears terrified him.

"I'm sure it will be fine," he said, his tone stiff suddenly.

"How can it be fine?"

"I only had one set of parents, and they were never particularly useful to me. Neither were they particularly loving. You seem to have two sets of parents who were quite fond of you. How can it not be fine?"

There was something strange about the way he said that, but then, there was something strange about the way he talked about emotion in general. The way he talked about connections with people, or the lack of them. She had noticed that the day they danced in the ballroom. It made her sad. Almost.

"I don't know how to face this. I don't know how to handle any of this. A week ago I was just Briar Harcourt. And now I'm...I guess I'm a long-lost princess."

"You were found," he said. "You are not lost anymore."

She didn't say, as she took hold of his arm and allowed him to lead her toward the double doors of the ballroom, that she felt more lost now than she ever had. No, she kept that observation to herself. And then the doors opened, and they walked out to the top of the stairway, where they were announced as Prince Felipe and Princess Talia. It was strange, and it felt somewhat detached, since the name still didn't feel like her own. But as they descended the stairs the sense of fantasy faded. And she felt the moment as sharp and real as anything had ever been.

Strange, because this was something out of a movie. Strange, that it was the first moment that felt truly real in the past week. Or maybe it was just the events catching up to her. The undeniable reality of the whole thing. The fact that if it was a dream she would have woken up by now, and she could no longer pretend that she might.

Then she saw them. Well, she saw Queen Amaani. A near mirror image of herself. A beautiful, dark-skinned woman standing there holding her husband, King Behrendt's, arm. She had a heavy golden crown on her dark hair, signifying her ranking.

The king himself had piercing blue eyes, a strong nose and neatly kept gray hair and beard. Clearly much older than his wife, he was still a handsome man, his presence announcing his status more clearly than a crown ever could.

Briar found herself clutching Felipe's arm as though without him she would collapse completely. It was a perverse thing, that she found herself leaning on his strength in this moment. She should push him away. She should push him away and run to her parents. But she was afraid that if she let go of him she would crumble to the floor.

The people in the ballroom blurred into indistinct shapes, the men a wave of black, the women a watercolor rainbow. All she could see was her mother and father. And Felipe. She could still see him. She could feel his warmth. Could feel his strength.

She swallowed hard as she approached the king and queen.

"Let us step out onto the balcony," Felipe said, leading the way, holding on to her as he led her through the crowd and out toward a large balcony that overlooked the gardens.

Nobody followed them, and then she realized that there were guards preventing anyone from leaving the ballroom and interrupting the reunion.

Suddenly, Briar found herself enveloped in her parents' arms. And that was when she lost hold of everything. Of her emotions. Of her control. And she let the tears fall.

There was nothing to say. Because it transcended words. She supposed that there would be time to ask about what had happened in the years since they had seen each other. Though she gathered quickly that they knew things like what she had majored in, and that they had been sent photographs all through her growing up. She was the one with the real deficit. The one who knew nothing of her past, the one who knew nothing of her family. Of her country, of the palace that she had once called home, of her half brothers and their wives and children.

But there would be time for all of that later. Because for now, there was nothing but this. But this deep, happy, devastatingly sad reunion that she had been waiting for all her life without even realizing it.

She looked up and saw Felipe studying them as though he was looking at something he simply couldn't understand. She shouldn't be looking at him now. Except, he had been instrumental in this reunion. But without his father she wouldn't have been given up in the first place. But then, she wouldn't have known the parents that she loved so dearly, the mother and father who had raised her. Everything was mixed up in her head and she didn't know how she felt anymore. Didn't know if she was happy, didn't know if she was sad. Didn't know if she was angry at that devastatingly handsome man standing apart from them, or if she felt sorry for him.

If she wanted to run from him, or if she wanted to draw closer to him.

"Sadly," he said finally, "we cannot stand out here all night."

King Behrendt looked up at Felipe, his expression stern. "Haven't you and your people robbed us of enough time already?"

"It is unfortunate," Felipe returned. "However, in the future you will have endless time to spend together. I do not intend to keep her from you. In fact, I intend to ensure that we have brilliant relations between our two countries. This is a reunion. Not simply for our families, but for the goodwill between Verloren and Santa Milagro. I understand that you might not appreciate the tactics. But Briar has agreed to marry me. I'm sorry, Princess Talia has agreed to marry me."

Queen Amaani looked stricken by the use of her other name. But she stepped forward. "Which name do you prefer?" she asked Briar, her voice soft.

"I don't know that I prefer either one," she said. "I'm just getting used to everything."

"We've always known what they called you," she said. "If that's what you want to be called, if you want to be Briar, you can be."

"I'll be Talia," she said, not sure if she meant it or not. But she didn't want to cause these people any more pain. Not after all they had been through.

"We can find another way," her father said, his expression hard as he looked at Felipe.

Briar shook her head, because she knew they couldn't. It was just that her father was too proud to acknowledge anything else. "You don't have to. I've been away for a long time. I haven't had the chance to be part of this. To be part of royal life. To serve my country in any way. This is how I can do it." She realized, as she spoke the words, that she meant them.

Her parents gave her one last lingering hug before they headed back into the ballroom, with promises to have her travel to Verloren as soon as possible, and promises to visit the palace in Santa Milagro often.

"I think," said Felipe, walking up slowly behind her, pressing his hand against her lower back, "that I will call you Briar."

It sent a strange, electric jolt through her. To have him touch her. To have him say that. She didn't know why that affected her. The thought that he would call her Briar.

"You don't have to," she said.

"I'm going to."

She stopped walking and turned to face him. He kept his hand planted firmly on her lower back. "And if I don't want you to?"

"I still will."

She frowned. "Why?"

He examined her closely, something in his dark eyes sharper, clearer than usual. It was then that she realized that lazy, indolent manner he sometimes threw over himself like a cloak was exactly that. Just something he put on.

She wondered about the real man. The one who wasn't a monster or Prince Charming. The man beneath all of that. Then, just as quickly as she wondered about that, she wondered if he even existed anymore. Or if he had been buried underneath a rock wall that he had carefully constructed around any and all authenticity.

"Because I should think you would like it if your entire past wasn't erased."

"It might be less painful." To just pretend that her childhood in New York, her family, her friends, didn't exist anymore. To pretend that Briar didn't exist anymore. That thought made her feel hollow.

"Life is painful," he said. "Loss is painful."

"You're acknowledging that I'm experiencing loss at your hand?"

"Circumstances are what they are. It doesn't have to be a loss. Unless… Did you have a lover back home?"

She shook her head. "If I did I never would have talked to you on the street in the first place." Maybe she should have lied. Maybe that would have been better. To make him think that she had another man in her life. But he would find out soon enough that it wasn't true. If he hadn't figured it out already. If this question wasn't just another piece of bait.

Because he seemed to know what she was feeling before she did. Seemed to understand what was happening in her body even when it mystified her.

"Because you felt it, too," he said, his voice like a touch, skimming over her entire body. Touching her in places no one ever had before.

She wanted to deny it. Wanted to pretend she had no idea what he was talking about. And she really didn't want to question what he meant when he said that she had felt it, too. As if he had felt something. Something other than the thrill of a hunter spotting his quarry.

She didn't want to get drawn into this. Didn't want to get drawn into looking at him and searching for humanity. It was much better if she only looked at the facade. If she only looked at the monster. Much better if she never tried to search behind that rock wall.

And yet she felt the pull, the tug toward him. The undeniable need to understand him. Maybe that wasn't so bad. Maybe it wasn't so dangerous. To try and understand the man she would supposedly spend the rest of her life with.

"What did you feel?" she asked. "When you saw me."

"You were beautiful. I responded to that. I'm a man, after all."

"There are a lot of beautiful women."

"Yes. But there are very few women who represent payment for an outstanding debt owed to my country." Something shifted in his expression. He was so difficult to read. His moods seeming to shift like sand without giving any warning. "Did you know my father had renounced marriage at the point when he announced he would claim you? He did not intend to take you as a wife. He intended to make you a mistress. On your sixteenth birthday."

Horror pierced through her. "He did?" She blinked rapidly. "But what about your…? What about your mother?"

"At that point she was dead. And anyway he never cared about her. He had mistresses all through their marriage. He paraded them about the palace whenever he saw fit. Women who were younger, women who weren't made weary by a lifetime of abuses and indignities. And he made sure that my mother knew they were infinitely more desirable than she would ever be. He made sure to let her know that she was a failure. For a great many reasons, though I was one of them. She never could keep me in line. Never could keep me in my place. My father demanded that one small thing from her, and she couldn't do that, either. And so he made her life hell. In part because he enjoyed doing it. In part because of me."

"He…he showed you that sort of thing was normal," she said, wondering how he'd ever had a hope of developing a conscience.

"Yes. But I knew they weren't. I knew that intending to take a woman some forty years younger than him—not a woman, a girl!—and make her his plaything was wrong. I never intended to use women that way. I never intended to use you that way. But I did recognize that you would be useful. That your symbolism could be changed."

"How very strange. Because I have never felt like a symbol. I've only ever felt like a girl."

"I'm well aware that you're neither of those things. You are not a symbol." He moved nearer to her, brushing the backs of his knuckles over her face. "You're far too warm. You're too alive. But also… You're not a girl. You're a woman."

For the first time, she felt like one. With his finger slowly drifting over her skin, those dark eyes pinning her into place, she didn't feel like a tall, awkward girl who was hopelessly different than everyone around her. Didn't feel like a simple curiosity. Didn't feel like a child in sophisticated clothes playing at something she was not.

No, in this moment, rooted to the spot, she felt every inch a woman. And she wanted to find out why that was. Wanted to respond to everything that was male in him and explore what it all meant. But it was all tangled up. Jumbled together with the reality of the situation. And then weighted down completely by the diamond on her finger, as if it were a millstone.

Perhaps she was simply succumbing to the insanity of the situation. Perhaps she had lost her mind completely.

Did it matter? That was the real question.

He let his fingertips drift down to the edge of her jaw then traced the line to the center of her chin. He tilted her face upward, his mouth a breath away from hers. She felt like she was being lifted off the ground. Her lungs, her body, filled completely. Expanding until she felt like she might burst with whatever feeling was taking her over. It was strange, and it was foreign. She wasn't entirely sure she liked it. Wasn't entirely sure she didn't.

"Your Majesty," a voice came from behind them.

Felipe dropped his hand and took a step back. "What is it?" he asked without ever taking his eyes off her.

"Prince Felipe. It's your father."

At that, Felipe turned and faced the man who had joined them on the terrace. "What is it?"

"The king is dead."

Something went horribly blank, flat in Felipe's eyes. She could feel ice radiating from his skin. He said nothing for a moment. And then, he tilted his face upward, his expression one of schooled arrogance, overlaid with a breathless lack of remorse.

Then he finally spoke, a strange smile curving his lips. "Long live the king."

CHAPTER SEVEN

"I SUPPOSE WE will be making more than one announcement tonight," Felipe said, his tone hard.

Then he straightened the cuffs on his jacket and walked back into the ballroom. Leaving Briar standing there by herself feeling utterly helpless. His reaction was frightening, and she didn't know what to do with it. Didn't know why she cared. Didn't know why it hit her quite so squarely in the chest and made it so hard for her to breathe.

Then she saw people begin pouring out of the ballroom. Heading back up the stairs, leaving the party much sooner than she was sure they had been planning. She lifted the front of her gown and hurried inside. She could hear Felipe shouting, but didn't understand what he was saying as he was speaking in Spanish.

Then he switched to English. "The party is over," he said. "My father is dead. I will be assuming the throne now. But we will not dance anymore tonight. Go home. Everybody get out."

And his word was obeyed for, after all, he was the king.

The only people who hesitated were her parents. She looked between Felipe and her mother and father, then she went to the king and queen. "You should go," she said, reaching out and placing her hand over her mother's.

"Are you certain you'll be all right?" the other woman asked.

She looked back at Felipe, who was standing there perfectly smooth and unruffled. She knew it was a lie. She just did. Whether or not it made any sense, she knew. This was another of his games. Another of his facades.

"Yes," she said. "I'll be fine. Leave me with him."

That left her in the ballroom, empty all except for herself and Felipe. And she realized that it had not been the moment she had accepted his proposal, not the moment he had placed the ring on her finger, that she had truly chosen this, chosen him. It was now.

She wasn't sure she would ever be able to explain why. Only that he needed her. He needed someone. She didn't know who else it would be.

The tables were still laden with food, and there was music being piped in over the speakers. But no one else was there. Not a single guest, not a single servant. With the chandelier glittering above and all the lights lit, casting the golden room in a fierce glow, it all seemed rather eerie. Particularly with the deep emotion radiating from the man who stood before her.

Apparently, she was with him. She had a feeling that she had been from the moment she'd first set eyes on him. Her world had shifted then. Regardless of what had happened since, in that moment…she had connected with him.

"Are you all right?"

He looked at her, the expression on his face indicating that he was surprised to find her still there. "Of course I am. Why wouldn't I be?" He straightened his sleeves, then his hands moved to the knot on his tie, and he straightened that, too, even though it hadn't been askew at all.

"Your father is dead."

"Yes. And I am now the king. And everything that I have wanted to do for the past two decades can now come to fruition. I'm more than all right."

He didn't look it. He didn't sound it.

"Felipe," she said, taking a step toward him.

He turned abruptly, gripping the edge of one of the tables that was laden with food, and he turned it over. She gasped and took a step back as glass shattered on the marble floor, champagne running through the tiles like a river.

"I feel better," he said. "Yes. I feel better."

"That was a waste of food."

"I'll make a donation. Around the time I make a donation that matches the cost of your ring. Do you find that acceptable?"

"I wasn't... I was just..."

"My father had not one quality to redeem him, Briar," Felipe said. "Not one. He victimized every person who walked through his life. And this—" he swept his hand to the side, indicating the mess he had just made "—would have appalled him. He could not abide disorder. Could not abide disorder while he created chaos inside everyone who lived underneath his roof. I always found that the greatest irony. He claimed he wanted everything to run smoothly while he ruined my mother from the inside out. Tell me, does that make any sense?"

She shook her head. "No."

"No. It doesn't. I will not make you miserable. I promise you." He began to pace, his movements agitated. He gripped the edge of his sleeve with his thumb and fore-finger and straightened it again. Then he repeated the action again. "Because it makes no sense. I'm not a soft man. I don't believe in love. I don't believe in romance. But I can certainly accomplish the amazing feat of not being a cruel bastard."

She stood where she was for a moment, not moving away from him, but not moving forward, either. She wasn't sure if another explosion of violence was going to come. She wouldn't be surprised if it did. He was all barely leashed energy and a strange kind of manic emotion that she had never seen before.

It turned out, she didn't have to move toward him at all. Because a moment later he was closing the distance between them. His dark eyes blazing into hers. And then, those eyes were all she saw. All she saw as he wrapped his arm around her waist and drew her hard up against his body.

She couldn't breathe. She didn't even have a moment to react. Because then, his mouth was crashing down on hers, his lips taking hers, consuming her. She had never been kissed before, so she didn't know what she had expected. But it hadn't been this. No, she never could have anticipated this, not in her wildest fantasies.

Because in her imagination a kiss had always been a sweet thing, romantic thing. In her fantasies, a kiss was meant to be shared with someone you loved, or at the very least someone you cared about. She couldn't claim that she cared about Felipe at all.

But that didn't seem to matter. Because while there wasn't…caring, there was something else. Something hot and reckless that burned through her like wildfire. And whatever he had been before, whatever she thought about him, was consumed by it, leaving behind nothing but ash. Making it impossible for her to remember how she had gotten here, and who she was. If she was Princess Talia, or Briar Harcourt. If she was a prisoner, a forced bride, or if she was kissing this man simply because he was the only man she had ever wanted.

For a moment she simply stood there, stood and marveled at the kiss. As his tongue slid over the seam of her lips, requesting entry. She didn't know what to do. Didn't know what she wanted. Her heart was thundering so hard she was certain that he could hear it. Certain that he could feel it butting up against his own chest as close as he was holding her.

Her arms were pinned to her sides, her hands curled into fists.

But then, his hold on her changed. He shifted, spreading his fingers, holding on to her in a way that was firm, sure and comforting in the oddest way. Then with his other hand he cupped the back of her head, tilting his head and granting himself access to her mouth, tasting her deeply.

After that she was lost. Completely and utterly. In the sensations that were pouring through her body like a liquid flame, in his heat, his presence, the strength of his body. And in the need that she hadn't realized her body was capable of feeling.

She had always thought she was somewhat dispassionate. After all, she had never even been tempted by the boys she had gone to university with. But that was the problem. The problem, which she had realized that first moment she had laid eyes on Felipe. They were boys. They were nothing but boys, and he was a man. A man who called to everything woman inside her. The man who made her realize that she was a woman.

The man who made her realize what a wonderful thing that was.

Her breasts ached, and he tightened his hold on her, crushing her up against that hard, muscular wall of his chest. She wanted him to touch her. Wanted his hands on her, not just this kind of passive contact that teased her with what she wanted without actually giving it.

As if he read her mind, he shifted, and instead of putting his hands on her he simply let her feel what she did to him. Let her feel the evidence of his own arousal, pressed up against her belly like an iron rod.

She had never been close enough to a man to experience anything like this. And she… She loved it. She was glorying in it. In the effect that she had on him. She didn't feel awkward. She didn't feel different. She felt *singular*. She felt *beautiful*. That she had the power to affect this man—this glorious, intoxicating man—in the way that she was… How could she feel anything but wholly, purely *desired*?

Except that he was the man who had kidnapped her. The man who had forced her into this engagement. Those thoughts swirled around in her mind along with the fog of arousal. She knew that she should grasp on to those little bits of sanity. But she didn't want to. She didn't want sanity. Not now. She just wanted this. This kind of reckless madness that she was certain would be her undoing.

But she was undone already, wasn't she? She had been cautioned all her life, told to be careful, and it was all because she was running from this man. But here she was, she was in his palace, she was in his arms, and he was consuming her. It was too late. She had been taken by the dragon, and she might as well give in to this, as well. There was nothing else that could be done. And in this moment, it seemed the most logical thing of all to give him this, too.

He growled, reversing their positions and pressing her back up against the wall. Against the windows that overlooked the garden outside. She knew that—despite the fact it seemed they were in isolation—there were still hundreds of people milling around the palace. She didn't care. She didn't care about anything. Nothing but this.

He moved his hands, dragging them down so that he was gripping her hips, his blunt fingertips digging into her skin. But she liked it. Loved that feeling of him anchoring her to the earth, because she still felt like she was in danger of floating away.

Then his hands moved upward, and he gripped the neckline on her dress, tearing the delicate fabric, exposing her breasts to his hungry gaze. She gasped, wrenching her mouth away from his, the breath dragged from her lungs in long, unsteady pulls.

"Felipe," she said, gasping his name, but he didn't seem to listen. Didn't seem to hear. He was like a man possessed—his dark eyes wild, desperation pouring from him in waves. This was the real man. It was, and she knew it. Shaken, unhinged, broken. Needing something that she wasn't certain she knew how to give. Something she wasn't sure she wanted to give.

She had only known him a week. And in that time she had pledged her life to him. But she had not fully known what it might mean to pledge her body to him, as well. She still didn't. But then he lowered his dark head, sucking one tightened bud deep into his mouth, groaning harshly as he did.

She lifted her hands, not sure if she was moving to hold him to her or push him away. Instead, she ended up threading her fingers through his dark hair, resting them there as he continued to lavish attention on her breasts. And she wondered, just for a moment, what sort of woman she was. She flashed back to those words he had spoken to her. Knowing that he was a monster, she still wanted him.

And seeing him like this now, she wanted him even more. She liked this man better than the playboy she had met the first day. Liked him more than the twisted, cynical prince who always seemed intent on scoring points off her. She liked him sharp, liked him dangerous, with rough edges that could easily cut her all the way down to the bone.

Or perhaps *like* wasn't the word. Perhaps it was something deeper than that. Something that cut through the loneliness of that careful childhood she'd led. That strange sense of isolation, of feeling wrong, feeling different, that had always followed her wherever she went.

No, *like* was not the correct word. She wasn't sure that she *liked* any of this. But it was driving her, creating a need inside her as quickly as it satisfied it.

She had spent her entire life fully in control. Of her actions, of her desires, of everything around her. Being so entirely without it was terrifying. Liberating. She should tell him to stop. She should want him to stop. She wasn't going to. She didn't want to.

She had a feeling she knew where this was going. She might be inexperienced, but she wasn't innocent of the way things went between men and women. Though she wasn't sure she had any way of knowing how she would withstand it. What the consequences might be for her. It was like helplessly clinging to a speeding train, unsure of whether she should ride it out or jump off. Unsure of which might do more damage.

"I have to," he said, his voice sounding frayed, tortured, as he tilted his head to the side, sliding his tongue down the column of her neck, all the way down to her collarbone and down farther still, tracing the outline of one tightened nipple. "I have to," he repeated again, tearing her bodice completely so that the whole front of her gown was gaping wide.

She clung to his shoulders, the glass against her back warm now from her body being pressed against it for the past few minutes. She looked beyond him, at the empty ballroom, still all lit up as though it was expecting a crowd. But it was just the two of them now. Just the two of them and the broken glass on the floor and whatever ghosts Felipe was contending with.

He took hold of the flimsy skirt of her gown, curling his fingers around it and tugging it upward, past her hips. Then he pressed one hand between her thighs, bold fingers moving beneath the waistband of her panties, and then on through her slick folds. She was wet for him. There was no hiding it. Not from him, not from herself.

What does that say about you, I wonder?

Those words rolled to her head again, and she pushed them away. It didn't matter what it said about her. She didn't care. She had always cared. Had always tried to be the perfect daughter. To do exactly what her parents had told her to do. To earn her position in their household. No, they had never acted as though she had to do that, but it didn't matter. She had put that weight there. Had done her best to follow their rules, had done her very best to succeed, to be a monument to all that they had poured into her.

This stood in antithesis to that.

This served her. The immediate. The moment. The physical, yawning need inside her. And whatever the consequences might be after, she couldn't bring herself to think of them now. Couldn't bring herself to care.

He pressed one finger inside her then drew it back out again, rubbing it over the sensitized bundle of nerves at the apex of her thighs. She gasped, letting her head fall back, and he took advantage of that vulnerable position, pressing a hot, openmouthed kiss to the tender skin on her neck.

And all the while he created wicked magic between her legs with his fingers. Made her feel things that she had never imagined possible. Things that she had certainly never managed to make herself feel, no matter how hard she'd tried on long, lonely nights in her bedroom. This was different. This was different because it was him. Because she had no control over what he might do next. Over how hard or soft he might touch her, how quickly he might stroke her, or when he would pull away again.

Then he growled, removing his hand and gripping her hips again, pressing her more firmly against the window. He took hold of one wrist and raised it up over her head, before going to collect the other, pinning that one down, as well, holding her fast with one hand.

He tried to hold her skirt in place with his free hand, but quickly became frustrated and wrenched the skirt to the side, rendering it nothing more than an expensive strip of silk. Her panties suffered the same fate. And she realized she was standing there wearing nothing but the facsimile of a dress in front of this man who might as well be a stranger.

But could he really be considered a stranger now? Now that he had touched her in the most intimate place on her body? Not when she had let him. Surely, they were more than strangers now.

He kissed her then, deep and hard, and she could feel him shifting against her, but it didn't click exactly what was happening until she felt something hot, blunt and hard pressing up against the entrance of her body. Her stomach went into a freefall, nerves assaulting her. Of course she had known where this was going.

She felt a shock of nerves, but then he was kissing her so long and deep, and her head felt dizzy with desire and pleasure. And nerves didn't matter anymore. Only how much she wanted him.

He flexed his hips upward, breaching the barrier there, a sharp, tearing sensation assaulting her, making her feel as though she couldn't breathe. He was too much. Too big. She was too full and it didn't feel good. She wiggled her hips, trying to get away from him, but she was trapped completely between the hard, uncompromising window, and the hard uncompromising man. And he was too far gone to realize that she was in distress.

He only gripped her harder, retreating from her body before he thrust back inside her again. Only this time, it didn't hurt quite so bad. This time, a part of her welcomed the feeling of fullness. He retreated again then returned to her. And with each thrust pleasure began to edge out pain. Desire consuming fear.

And then she gave herself up to it, to him. Opened herself to him, rolled her hips in rhythm with his movements. There was nothing gentle about it. Just like her first kiss—which had happened an astonishingly short time ago—this was void of the kind of sweetness and gauzy romance she had always imagined the act would contain.

But she didn't mourn it. Because she had never wanted anyone else. She wanted him. So how could it be anything other than perfect?

It was a messy kind of perfect. A broken kind of perfect. But as the pleasure built, deep and intense inside her, she realized she didn't care. He rolled his hips up against hers, and bliss broke over her like a wave on the rocks.

She just shook and rode it out. As she shuddered out her pleasure, turning her face into the curve of his neck, doing her best to hold back the tears that began to push against her eyes, pressure building to almost unbearable levels.

He tightened his hold on her, his thumb and fingers digging so hard into her wrists she was certain it would leave a bruise. And then, he let out a harsh, feral growl as he found his own release. He released his hold on her, burying his fingers into her massive curly hair and claiming her mouth in a kiss that mimicked the act they had just finished.

This was no sweet, silent afterglow. It was a conflagration that still raged on in spite of their release.

And when it was done, he took a step away from her, regarding her with wild, dark eyes. "You will spend the night in my bed tonight," he said, the words a command and not a request.

And then, he turned away from her, striding away from her, not offering her so much as a comforting touch.

In spite of the heat that was still coursing through her body, she shivered.

CHAPTER EIGHT

SHE HAD BEEN a virgin. And he had taken her against a wall—no, a window—with absolutely no finesse.

Then he had left her standing there in a tattered dress, the bright streaks of blue a shocking contrast to that smooth, brown skin. Her small, high breasts and that dark thatch of curls at the apex of her thighs exposed, her hair a dark halo around her face.

Had left her standing there with the command that she join him in his bed tonight, when the fact of the matter was no one should come anywhere near him tonight. And he shouldn't inflict himself on anyone.

What had been in his mind? Sending everyone away as he had? He had come into the ballroom, waiting for the surge of triumph to flood his veins. Waiting for a sense of completion. Waiting for his lips to form the words to an eloquent speech.

About dark ages rolling forward into the light. But instead he had cleared the room.

Instead, he had done what he seemed compelled to do from some dark place inside him that had purchase on his soul, that he seemed to have no control over, and that was to sabotage the moment. To break. To destroy.

And he still felt no relief. No sense of completion.

Nothing but an end. A dark, blank end that offered him nothing but more emptiness. Like a chasm had opened inside him, one that had always been there, but one he now had to admit might always be.

His father was dead. That was supposed to be the key.

But now he couldn't yell at the old man. Couldn't scream at him and demand answers. Could never shout at him about the fact it was his fault Felipe's mother was dead. How it was all his fault.

Felipe swallowed hard, trying to get a handle on himself, on his control. This control he had long prized so much. He should not have Briar come to his room. He should deal with his demons alone.

But he would have her again. Because there was no other choice. Because the hollow feeling inside him was threatening to consume him, and the only moment of peace he'd had since his father's aide had come and announced the old man's death had been when he was buried in Briar's tight, welcoming heat.

It occurred to him as he flung open the doors to his chamber that she might not come. That she might go back to her room. Might hide from him.

She should. There was no question about that.

But if she did he would go after her.

There was also no question about that.

With shaking hands, he poured himself a glass of whiskey then stared down at the amber liquid. He was dangerous enough as it was. Unsteady, unstable. Disorderly. There was no greater sin in his father's eyes and there never had been.

The thought made a smile curve his lips. He might have wasted some opportunities tonight, but he had rebelled in a rather spectacular fashion. His father had prized all that surface order. Never mind if beneath the surface everything was jagged and destroyed.

Destroying the ballroom appealed to that part of him that wanted to wound the old man still. That hoped his ghost had watched the whole thing.

He looked down at the glass. As on edge as he was he wasn't entirely certain he should add alcohol to the equation. For Briar's sake and for no other reason. And so, he tilted the glass to the side before cocking his arm back and flinging it against the wall.

"I imagine that's a bit too disorderly for you as well, Father," he said.

There was every chance the old man could hear him. That he was now haunting the halls like the malevolent spirit he had always been. It would be fitting. This palace was full of ghosts; Felipe had never thought differently, no matter that his father had tried to tell him otherwise.

He was failing again. Which seemed to be what he did. Failing at not being a horror to the woman he was intent on taking as his wife. But then, he wasn't sure he was capable of being anything other than this. Anything other than the creature his father had set out to create.

He gripped the edge of the bar, lowering his head. He had to be different. He had to. If for no other reason than for Santa Milagro. His people had lived in darkness long enough.

Of course, he had no idea how he was supposed to remedy that when he feared he had no light inside him.

Then the door to his bedchamber opened and he lifted his head, turning it to look behind him. It was Briar. She was no longer wearing the shredded ball gown that he had left her in downstairs. She had changed into a long, flowing robe in a luminous pink that contrasted beautifully with her smooth, dark skin. She had washed her makeup off, leaving her looking young and freshly scrubbed. He had to wonder if she had been so eager to wash his touch from her body.

But she was here. And he felt almost certain she had brought some light in with her. Perhaps that was the key. Perhaps she was the key to more than he had originally imagined.

He ignored the slight twisting feeling in his chest that questioned this reasoning. That forced images of his mother to swim before his mind's eye.

"You came," he said.

"Yes," she said, scanning the room slowly, her eyes falling to the broken glass and spilled alcohol on the floor. "Clearly you can't be trusted around food at the moment."

"I can't be trusted around you, either," he said, his tone hard. "And yet, here you are."

She clasped her hands in front of her, wringing her fingers. "You asked me to come."

"I confess, I thought I might have to go retrieve you from the depths of your room. I thought I might have frightened you."

She lifted one elegant shoulder. "I'm not frightened of you."

He narrowed his eyes. "Truthfully?"

She released her hold on her hands, one fluttering slightly as she made a dismissive gesture. "Well. I suppose I am afraid of you. But not enough to hide from you."

"Is that because you've accepted your fate or because you find yourself fascinated by me?" The answer was important.

She frowned, a small dent growing between her eyebrows. "I think it took you stealing me away from the city for me to think I could do anything other than accept my fate, actually. And when I say that, it isn't because my life was terrible. I don't mean it in that way. It's just that it seemed predetermined. Like the path had been set since the beginning of my life. And then you showed me that I had no idea. None at all. I didn't know where I had started, and I had no idea what was out there, what was hunting me—so to speak. I would say that never in my life have I been at a point where I was more likely to accept the way things are than I am right now. And yet, here I am."

Something shifted inside him, a rumble of satisfaction beginning in his chest, growing. "Perhaps because I was your first man?"

Color tinged her cheeks. "You could tell?"

"Yes."

"And you did it anyway?" She tilted her head to the side, a strange expression on her face.

"It wasn't forefront in my mind. It was afterward. If I had stopped and thought about it while it was happening, I would have realized. As it was, I didn't put everything together until it was too late."

She looked somewhat appeased by that. "Okay."

"Does it matter to you?"

"I don't know if it matters. Well, yes, it does. I wouldn't like to think that it meant nothing to you. I have never wanted a man before. I wasn't a virgin because I was waiting for anything. I mean, nothing moral. I wasn't waiting for you, or some other mythological husband. I was just waiting for somebody that I wanted. I was waiting for the moment I didn't want to say no. And that happened downstairs with you. I don't know why.

I just know that it was different. That it changed something in me. So yes, if it meant nothing to you I would find that painful."

He felt a smile touch the corner of his lips. He walked toward her, closing the distance between them. Then he reached out, pressing his thumb against the center of her lower lip. "You want to be special to me, *querida*?"

She trembled beneath his touch, her dark eyes questioning. Searching. She wouldn't find anything. Not in him. Nothing but more darkness. That endless, blank pit that existed in his chest. Selfishly, he wanted her answer to be yes. And yet, he knew that he should want nothing from her. And he should rejoice if she wanted nothing from him.

Still, he waited. And he hoped. A strange, costly thing for a man like himself. To reach for a flame, wondering if it was going to warm him, or if the action would simply snuff it out.

"That's not so shocking, is it?" she asked, her voice hushed. "We... We were intimate with each other. Of course I want it to matter."

"Intimate?" He could honestly say he had never considered sex intimate. It was a release. It was bodies, only bodies. And long ago he had determined to detach himself from his body when he needed it to be so. To be able to make it so he felt no pain while undergoing excruciating torture.

To feel nothing but pleasure when he was in the arms of a woman—no matter what he might feel inside.

A body was simply that. Fallible, temporary. Losing himself in someone else's had never felt like anything more than pleasure.

And yet she called it intimacy. She had never wanted

another man. Had never allowed another man to touch her. He was not sure if he knew how to make someone special to him, but it seemed that he might be special to her.

He was equally at a loss as to what he was supposed to do with that.

But it satisfied him. Satisfied something inside him he had not known existed until that very moment. It was the deepest kind of satisfaction, satiating him in a way his orgasm hadn't even managed to.

"Yes," she said, her voice soft. She lifted her hand, pressed it flat against his chest. "What we did was intimate. Something that you don't share with just anyone." She frowned. "Or do you?"

"I have," he said, with no shame at all. "Desire exists to be satisfied."

"I don't think that's true. I think what makes desire matter is that it can't be satisfied in any time. What makes it so deep is that it's reserved only for certain people. For certain moments."

He wrapped his fingers around her wrist, held her hand more firmly against his chest. "As the woman who just confessed to having never felt it before? You say that, but what if it were another man to fire these feelings inside you? If it were to happen again, would you simply accept his advances as you did mine?" The thought was like acid, eating through his mind and sliding on down to his chest where it began to burn around the edges of the blackness there.

She shook her head. "No."

"So that makes me important?" He tightened his hold on her. "That means I'm important to you."

He never had been. Not to anyone. Not to his cruel,

sadistic father or his broken, fragile mother. He wanted it. More desperately than he had ever wanted anything, and he didn't care what that meant. Because he only understood want in a very singular way. Wanting was having as far as he was concerned. So he would have this. And he would feel no compunction about it.

"I said I would marry you," she said, looking away from him. "But you never answered if I was important to you."

"I said I would marry you," he said, parroting her words back to her. "Do you see any other women around here wearing my ring?"

She shook her head.

"There's your answer," he said. And then, the phone in his pocket vibrated. He said a curse then took it out, looking at the screen.

It was Rafe. The bastard really did have lousy timing. Why had he decided to have friends?

"We didn't get a chance to speak tonight," his friend said. "You threw everyone out of the palace."

"I'm surprised you left without being forced," he said to his friend, all the while keeping his eyes on Briar.

"Oh, Adam and I were forced," Rafe returned. "Though Adam was forced by his bride, who felt that your wishes should be respected. Because she simply doesn't know you well enough to know when you should be ignored."

"And what's your excuse?"

"I didn't suppose, given the disadvantage of my lack of sight, that I should engage your royal guards in a fight."

Felipe laughed. "Please. We both know you still had the advantage in the fight, Rafe."

"True enough."

"I assume that Adam was involved in this goodwill mission. You checking on my mental well-being." He took that moment to look at Briar more fully, to allow his gaze to travel over her beautiful curves. To truly relish just how flimsy that nightgown she was wearing was. He needed this phone call to be short.

"Your father has passed away. It isn't a small thing."

"It's better that he's dead. It was a cruelty of fate that he drew breath for as long as he did. There are a very great number of people who die far too young and don't deserve it."

"They say the good die young," Rafe pointed out.

"Then you and I are both safe."

"We are that," Rafe said, his tone hardening slightly. "We are that. I should be dead already. And likely would be if I were worthy of life."

Rafe's cynicism was one of the many reasons Felipe counted him a friend, when in general he found friendship to be pointless.

"Right now I'm grateful to be alive. I outlived that old bastard—" his gaze returned to Briar "—and I have a promising evening before me."

"You're with your fiancée, I assume," Rafe said.

"Yes. So you'll understand that I have to cut this call short."

"A word of caution," Rafe said. "This woman you have… I did a bit of research. And Adam described her to me. She is too soft for you, my friend. Far too young."

"Very much," Felipe returned, his eyes never leaving Briar, who was blushing beneath his frank appraisal. "She's too innocent for me, as well."

Her gaze sharpened, her mouth dropping open as she

realized she was the topic of discussion. She, and her virginity.

"That's even worse," Rafe said. "You have to be careful with women like that."

Felipe laughed. "Please. I spent my entire childhood at the mercy of a sadistic old man. I'm not in any danger."

"That makes it even clearer to me that you might be. Men like you and me… We can't be broken by the hard things. It's the soft things. Believe me. I know of what I speak."

Rafe had never given the details of how he lost his eyesight. All he and Adam knew was that there had been an accident. But Felipe had long suspected a woman had been involved in some capacity. This… This confirmed it. Except, Felipe had a difficult time imagining his friend falling prey to a woman, no matter how soft or beautiful she was.

"I'll keep that in mind." He hung up then. He wouldn't be keeping it in mind. Not tonight. Tonight he wanted only one thing. And as he advanced on his beautiful fiancée, he could think only that she had much more to be afraid of than he did.

"You were talking about me," she accused.

"Yes."

"Who was it?"

"A friend."

"You have friends?" Her eyes widened. If it wasn't objectively such a surprising thing that he had friends, even to him, he might have been offended. Instead, he found himself amused.

"I do. Two of them. And to answer your question, yes, they have myriad issues. Definitely not normal."

"I suppose I'm not normal, either."

He wrapped his arm around her waist, drew her up against his chest. "I don't need you to be normal. I need you to be mine."

She looked at him, marveled at him as though he were some kind of curiosity. Something she had never seen before, and was trying to figure out. Then she lifted her hand, drawing her fingertips lightly across his cheek.

He growled, taking hold of her wrist again and holding her steady as he brought his lips down to hers. As he claimed a kiss that he needed more than his next breath.

And then, Rafe didn't matter at all. Neither did the ghosts of his past. The ghost of his father that was likely rattling chains and wandering restlessly down the halls even now.

Nothing mattered but this. But her. But her beauty, her delicacy. The fact that he should stay away from her, because she would be so easily bruised, crushed like a delicate rose.

Perversely, he wanted it. Wanted to see the effect that he had on her. Wanted to ruin her. To make her his. Like he had wanted to ruin everything in this whole damn palace from the moment he had found out his father was dead. Disorder. That was what he wanted. Utter chaos. And he would be the king of it.

That drove him on. Spurred him to deepen the kiss. To crush his mouth against hers, to swallow the sounds she made, whether they were of pleasure or protestation, he wasn't entirely sure. But he was consumed by this. Consumed by his need for her.

He knew nothing else, and that was a blessed relief. He opened his eyes, looked at his own hands, holding on to her face, at his sleeves. Those damn sleeves. He released his hold on her, wrenching his jacket off, then working at the buttons of his shirt before he cast it to the ground, as well.

He hadn't been naked the last time they had been together. Hadn't felt those soft, sweet hands pressed up against his skin. Well, he needed it now. Needed it more than he needed his next breath. And as much as he wanted her to be marked by him, he wanted the same in return.

"Touch me," he demanded, his voice rough, a stranger's voice. He had learned to conduct himself with the manner of a gentleman. Had learned how to be suave, how to be smooth. How to cover up the monster inside by pretending to be a man of impeccable manners.

That was gone now. Cast to the ground with his clothes. Shattered like the glass he had broken against the wall. She already knew. She knew he wasn't that. That he never could be. Because he had shown her the truth. And she was still here. Said that she still wanted him. That she wanted to mean something to him.

Foolish girl. Inexperienced *girl*. She was everything that Rafe had said. Too soft. Too innocent. Too young.

But he was his father's son.

He pushed that thought to the side. He didn't want to examine it, not now. Couldn't. There was no possibility of thought, not now.

His father was dead anyway. And all the duplicity he had lived under, the extreme control, the calculated air of not caring at all…it was dead with him.

He didn't need it anymore.

He was king now. And he would do as he wished.

Inexperienced fingers brushed against his throat, moved down his chest. "Like you mean it," he growled, his lips against hers as he issued the rough command.

Her touch grew firmer, a bit more confident, and she dragged her fingertips down his washboard-flat stomach, to the waistband of his pants. "Yes," he said, the word rough and encouraging. "Like that."

She fumbled with his belt, and he clung to her as she pushed his pants down his thighs, taking his underwear with it. Leaving him completely naked standing in front of her. He watched her expression closely, tried to read her thoughts. It seemed as though she didn't know where to look, her dark eyes darting every which way as she examined his body.

"Have you never seen a naked man before?" Oh, he liked that. Liked this far too much. That he was corrupting her. That he was altering her in ways that were irreparable.

She shook her head. "I mean, in pictures."

"You've never undressed anyone. Never touched them. Never watched a man get hard because of you."

"No," she said. "Until you I had never been kissed."

Without being conscious of making the decision to do so, he found himself closing the distance between them. Growling as he took her into his arms and kissed her with all the uncivilized ferocity inside him.

She whimpered, her hands trapped between them, her palms resting on his chest. He was hard, throbbing and insistent against her body, and he knew that she could feel it. That she could feel just how affected he was by her. Just how much he wanted her. There was nothing civilized about this. But perhaps, just maybe, it was intimate. Because this was beyond him in a way that sexual desire had never been before.

This seemed to be tangled up in emotions in a way

that the need for release never had been. And it had been
so from the moment he had taken her downstairs. When
he had turned that table over, ripping the mask of the
civilized prince off and letting the monster free. He had
done that. In front of her. For her. Almost because of her.
It was as though she reduced his control in ways that he
could scarcely understand. Ways he certainly had not
given permission for.

But strangely, she didn't seem to fear him. Didn't seem
to fear that at all.

None of it made sense. That she would be the one to
see that side of him, and yet not be afraid. That he would
be the one to make her desire for the first time, when he
was little more than a villain to her. The man who had
ripped her from her life and dragged her into this. Into
his domain.

But he didn't need sense. Not now.

"Now," he said, the words pulled from him, "you have
been kissed."

She nodded, her kiss-swollen mouth soft, completely
irresistible. And he leaned in to devour her again. It made
no sense. That she was so receptive to this. To him. She
should be disgusted by him. By the beast he had trans-
formed into from the moment he had brought her back
here to the palace. Or rather, from the moment he had revealed to her his intentions to take her back to his country.

But then he supposed that he should be disgusted by
those things, as well. He wasn't.

He needed her. Needed her to rule his country in the
best way. And more than that, now he wanted her. Wanted
her in his life, in his bed. Wanted to be inside her. He
would not deny himself.

And so, he could feel no guilt.

"Shall I teach you something?"

She looked up at him, her dark eyes luminous. Then she licked her full lips. "Yes. Teach me."

CHAPTER NINE

HIS HEART THUNDERED HARD, the blood firing through his veins hot and fast. He drew himself away from her. "Get down on your knees for me."

"The floor is hard," she said, her expression blank.

"That is true," he said, sweeping her up into his arms and crossing into his bedchamber. "We shall make it a bit more comfortable for you." He set her down in front of his bed, on the plush rug there. "Will this be a little more gentle on your royal knees?"

She blinked. "I…"

He cupped her chin, gazed into her eyes. "Kneel for me."

She complied, and he had to close his eyes, grit his teeth tight, to keep from coming then and there. She hadn't even touched him, but that simple act of compliance did more for him, did more to him, than a thousand illicit acts before had ever done.

"Take off that gown," he said, indicating the belt that held her robe closed. "I need to see you."

With shaking fingers, she undid the knot, let the silken fabric slide down her shoulders. And there she was, naked before him on her knees, her black hair tumbled over her shoulders, her sleek curves so enticing it took all his control to keep himself from lifting her back up into his arms and tumbling her onto the bed. To keep himself from burying himself inside her body again, and forgetting these little power games.

It occurred to him then, that if she was a virgin it was entirely possible she wasn't on any sort of birth control. He had taken her earlier without a condom, and he had no intention of using one this time, either. The idea of her pregnant, growing round with his child, only sent another shock of satisfaction through him. Then she would truly be bound to him. Forever.

She would not be able to leave. At least, not easily.

Ah, yes, your father's son.

He pushed the thought away again as he tangled his fingers in her hair and drew her toward his body. "Take me in your mouth," he said.

She looked up at him, uncertainty on her face. Perhaps she would reject him now. And perhaps, that was what he had been pushing her toward the entire time. Maybe that was what he wanted. To find her breaking point. To find the point at which she would become disgusted with him. For it had to exist. The fact that she had wanted him up until this point made no sense to him.

But, she did not pull away. Instead, she adjusted her position, lifting her hand and curling her fingers tentatively around his length. Then she leaned forward, her slick tongue darting out over the head of his arousal before she slowly took him inside her mouth.

And then, whatever he had imagined might happen, whatever guidance he thought he might give, was lost completely. There was nothing. His mind was blank and his body was on fire. She had absolutely no skill, was

clearly not a woman who had ever touched a man before, and yet, it was the most erotic experience of his life.

Because it was just for him. As she had said. It was an
intimacy. It was special. And that mattered. It mattered
to a man who had never had such a thing before. A man
who had never even known to hope for such a thing. She
wanted him. She wanted him when she had wanted no
other man before him.

She gave to him, generously. Gave him far more than
he deserved. Those inexpert hands moving in rhythm
with her lips and tongue as she lavished pleasure on him.
Like a woman would do for her beloved, not for her kidnapper.

Not for a man who had commanded she get down on
her knees and give him pleasure as though it was his due.

And then, he was no longer able to control himself. He
tightened his fingers in her hair, pulled her head back.
"Not like this," he said.

She rocked back on her heels, wobbling, and he caught
her by the wrist, drawing her up against his body and
claiming her mouth in a searing kiss.

He tumbled her backward onto the bed, groaning
loudly as every inch of her naked body pressed against
every inch of his. She was impossibly soft. Refined. Delicate. Lovely beyond measure.

Not for him.

And he felt… He felt like a criminal, getting away
with the perfect crime. Which was   he discovered in
that moment—an intensely satisfying feeling. To be in
possession of something far too lovely, far too fine, for
a man such as himself.

Perhaps other men might feel guilt.

He was not other men.

He was a monster. And she knew it. She wanted him still.

He groaned, lowering his head, taking one tightened nipple between his lips and sucking hard. She arched beneath him, a raw sound on her lips.

"Why do you want me?" he asked, the question surprising even himself, the words broken, torn from a part deep inside himself he had not known existed.

She looked at him, her dark eyes glazed, her expression full of confusion. "What?"

"You're too good. You're too soft. Why do you want me? It doesn't make any sense. You should be disgusted by me. Don't you understand that? I'm not a good man. You are a good girl. A very good girl. Soft and fragile. Protected. Protected from monsters like me. And yet, here you are, flinging yourself at me. It makes no sense."

"You asked for me," she said simply. "That's hardly me flinging myself at you."

He growled, taking her other nipple into his mouth and sucking on her until she gasped, until she arched against him again. And then, he released her. "There you are. Flinging yourself at me. And I need to know why."

"Did it ever occur to you that it's because you're everything I don't have? You're hard, where I'm soft. Dangerous. And I've been so protected, just like you said. And you are… Well, you're a bit bad, aren't you?"

She lifted her hand, touched the side of his face, and he turned, grazing her fingertip with his teeth. "Just a bit."

"Maybe I've been just a little bit too good, then. Maybe people need both, and I don't have any of my own. So, I need some of yours."

He rolled his hips against hers, felt slick, receptive

flesh beneath his unyielding hardness. "You need my darkness," he said.

She gasped, grabbing hold of his shoulders. "Yes."

He needed her light. Dammit, but he needed it. He wouldn't say it, not now. Couldn't say it. Because he was too consumed by the need to be inside her.

He pressed the head of his arousal against her entrance, slid inside inch by excruciating inch, torturing them both with that slow penetration. Belatedly, he was concerned that she might be sore. But he banished those concerns quickly enough. They paled in comparison to his need. His need to have her. To consume her in the way she was consuming him.

To have her light.

Darkness had been his constant companion, but right now he felt like he was standing on the edge of an abyss that was something beyond darkness. And only she was keeping him from falling completely.

He lost himself in her, burying his head against her neck as he chased that white-hot flame of release that he could only find in her. She grabbed hold of him, her fingernails digging into his skin, sounds of pleasure escaping her lips as she met his every thrust with one of her own.

Then she grabbed hold of his arms, a raw scream on her lips as she found her own release, her fingernails scraping a long trail down his forearms, all the way to the backs of his hands.

Marks from their encounter he wouldn't be able to hide. Disorder. Beautiful chaos. Found within his princess.

No. His queen.

And as she convulsed around him, he gave in to his

own release, flinging himself into the darkness. Because he knew that her light would be there when he reached the bottom.

The next few days passed in a flurry of activity. Briar scarcely saw Felipe in the light of day. But at night… Yes, she saw him at night. It didn't matter if she retreated to her own room, in that case, he would come and find her. He would find her, and he would make love to her for hours. Tapping into parts of herself she hadn't known existed.

But in the morning he was always gone. She had a suspicion that he never fell asleep with her. But rather, waited for her to drift off before succumbing himself.

It was times like this she felt her isolation keenly. The separation from her mother. If she was back in New York she could talk to Nell about this. Well, in some vague terms. She wouldn't go talking about everything they'd done in detail.

Her cheeks heated.

She wasn't quite sure how she had found herself in this situation. Bonding—physically at least—with the one man she should be most distant from.

When she tried to think of her life before Felipe, before coming here, it all seemed hazy. She supposed that wasn't a good sign. That for some reason these past weeks in Santa Milagro seemed bolder, more colorful, than the life before she had arrived here ever had.

She wondered if it was a trick, too. Some magical spell that Felipe had over her, even though she didn't believe in magic. Or rather, she hadn't before discovering she was a princess, and being spirited away to a foreign country by a prince that was far too handsome and far too wicked for anyone's good.

The very strange thing, though, was the fact that even though she had stepped into this life that was entirely unknown to her, had stepped into a role she had never imagined she might fulfill, she felt more herself than she ever had.

And it wasn't just because she had been happily creating art programs, working out grants and funding for various schools and cataloging the artwork long forgotten in the years since King Domenico had shuttered the museums.

Art had always made her feel alive, it was true, but it was more than that. Perhaps it was because Felipe seemed to require nothing from her other than that she stand by his side, and that she make herself available to him when he had need of her body.

Otherwise, he didn't want a particular sort of behavior from her. At least, not that he'd said. There was no pressure to present herself as something perfect or demure, not when she was in his presence. He liked to push her, and he seemed to enjoy when she provided him with a spirited response.

He certainly seemed to enjoy that in the bedroom. Thinking of it even now made her cheeks heat. She pressed the back of her hand against the side of her face, cool skin pressing against hot, making her shiver.

She was currently digging through a room in the back of the palace that seemed to have been abandoned. There were a great many artifacts that she wanted cataloged for the museums, and she was doing her best to sort through what she might have different appraisers come and have a look at, and what probably didn't have any value beyond the sentimental.

She had been doing a lot of historical research on her adopted country, trying to give context to all the various pieces she was discovering. It seemed that the poor nation had only experienced pockets of peace and prosperity, while mostly enduring long stretches of time with kings who were tyrants.

But the people had created beautiful things, even during their oppression. Almost most especially during their oppression.

In the palace she had mostly found personal collections. Portraits of past rulers and their relatives, pieces of the crown jewels, which had been stowed in a very secure vault. She would prefer they be on display than sitting in the back growing tarnished. Felipe seemed to have no opinion on the matter, so she was proceeding.

But in the rooms she had discovered only yesterday, it was different. The jewelry was not cataloged. It was not organized at all. And yet, it seemed to be of amazing quality. Millions of dollars in gems hidden in drawers. Beautiful paintings—still life and portraiture—hidden behind canvas. Hand-carved furniture beneath tarps.

She let out a long, slow breath and dragged one large tarp off a piece that sat against the back wall. Her eyes widened as she looked over the beautiful chest of drawers. Different pieces of wood were inlaid to create a representation of the mountainous skyline visible from the windows here in the tower.

Thin strips of gold separated the different pieces of wood, and she had a feeling it was real precious metal. She brushed her fingertips over the mountain peaks, over the sun, positioned in the upper left-hand corner of the bureau.

There was so much hidden beauty here. She couldn't help but think it might be a metaphor for the man she was going to marry. She paused for a moment, Felipe's handsome face swimming before her mind's eye.

He was such a puzzle. Charming and smooth one moment, then rough and out of control the next. He seemed to crave order, his appearance never anything but perfectly polished. And yet, the night his father had died he had laid everything in his wake to ruin, including her.

She felt her cheeks grow even hotter.

What a ruin it had been.

She took a fortifying breath and turned away from the chest of drawers, making her way across the room to a shapeless mass covered by canvas that she assumed was more framed paintings of various sizes. She dragged the canvas down and was rewarded with exactly that.

Landscapes in gilt-edged frames, a painting of fruit on a table. She enjoyed looking at this sort of thing. Because it proved that people had always been people. Compelled to capture the things around them. Compelled to take some kind of snapshot of their dinner for the world to see.

She carefully moved the first couple of paintings to the side and paused when she saw a portrait of a woman she had never seen before.

She was beautiful. Her black hair was swept up into an elegant bun, a golden crown on her head. Her crimson lips were curved into a half smile, one that seemed to contain wicked secrets. It reminded her of... Well, it reminded her of Felipe.

"What are you doing?"

She jumped, turning at the sound of Felipe's voice.

"Just exploring the rooms. I'm handling the art, as we discussed. Getting everything ready for the museums."

"That isn't art," he said, his voice taking on a strange tone.

She frowned. "It is a painting."

"It's my mother," he said, swift and hard.

She looked between him and the painting, speechless for a moment. "I...I can see it, actually."

He laughed. "Can you? I had thought that she and I bore no resemblance at all."

"You do," she said softly, not sure if it was the right thing to say. She couldn't read his mood. But then, she so rarely could. Trying to grasp Felipe's motivations or feelings was a lot like grabbing hold of a handful of sand. You could wrap your fingers around it for a moment, but then it all slid away into nothing.

"I would prefer if her things stayed here," he said.

"I didn't realize these were your mother's things."

He nodded once. "Yes. I think they have been in here untouched since the day she died."

"How old were you when she died?"

"Seven," he said, his tone detached now.

He crossed the room, making his way over to the window. It had bars over it, she had noticed earlier. She had thought very little of it then, because often windows that were so high up had a precaution of some kind in place so that no accidents happened. But for some reason, when he made his way there, when he pressed his fingers against the pane of glass, she wondered about them.

"She died here," he said, the words conversational.

"Was she... Was she ill?"

"In a manner of speaking. She was not well, that's certain."

She didn't say anything. If there was one thing she had learned about Felipe—and she had actually learned several—it was that if he wanted to say something he would eventually. And if he didn't, there was no amount of pushing that would get him to speak. There were other ways of dealing with him that were much more effective.

She took a moment to think about those ways, curling her fingers into fists as she imagined running her palms over his face. It would be rough now, because it was late in the day and dark stubble covered his jaw. She liked that. Liked when he was a bit unshaven. A bit feral.

She liked herself that way, too. Which was surprising, she had to admit.

He pressed his palms flat against the window, and she noticed his gaze dropped to his shirtsleeves. But she didn't speak then, either. She was collecting bits of information about him. Had been from the moment she had first laid eyes on him. He fascinated her. He called to something deep inside her that she couldn't explain, not really. Except that… He seemed to need her. And in every other situation in her life, she had needed those around her.

It wasn't a bad thing. It was just that she'd had to make sure she behaved, make sure she was good so that she could somehow make her presence worthwhile.

He had needed her so badly he had kidnapped her. And perhaps there was some kind of twisted logic trying to make that a good thing, but then again, maybe there was no logic at all.

Maybe it was all just a feeling, and that was okay, too.

"My cuffs weren't straight," he said.

She looked down at them now, saw deep scratches

extending from them now, lending him a look that was much less than civilized. Marks she'd left on him.

Marring his perfection. Making a mockery of hers.

She felt her face heat.

"What?" She found herself taking a step toward him.

"That was the start of it. I was never quite so orderly as my father would have me be. And he took it out on my mother. He demanded perfection that could never be achieved, particularly when he himself was creating chaos beneath the surface." Felipe tapped the glass then turned to face her. "I did not have a nanny. My father demanded that my mother care for me. Otherwise, what was her use?"

"How did you… How did you know about all of this? It doesn't seem right that a little boy should have heard all this going on between his parents."

He flashed that wicked smile, but there was no joy behind it. "That was never a concern. In fact, my father demanded I bear witness to all manner of indecency he subjected my mother to. If I misbehaved and she had to be slapped across the face, he wanted me to see it. And vice versa. He much preferred punishing her for my sins and me for hers. You see, it's so much more painful to watch your mother be struck because you spoke at a moment when you should not have than it is to be hit yourself." He looked back at the window. "She was always quite delicate. Like a bird. She escaped him. She flew away."

"She left him?" Briar asked, searching for clarity.

"She jumped out the window." He wrapped his knuckle against the glass. "That's why there are bars. I suppose my father didn't want to lose another family member in the same way. It would begin to reflect poorly on him."

He said the words so dispassionately, and Briar found

herself unable to breathe through the grief that exploded in her chest like a bomb. For his mother. For him. It seemed unfathomable that a small boy should lose his mother that way.

It seemed equally unfathomable that the woman in that portrait, the woman who had most certainly started out with as much spark in life as Felipe himself had, could have been reduced, tormented, until she felt that was her only escape.

"Felipe... I'm so sorry. I don't understand how he got away with that. With tormenting you both. What did the public think?"

"That it was an unfortunate accident. And of course, my father controlled the press. And no one would ever question what he had decreed."

"So no one knew. No one has ever known."

"No," he said, his tone hard. "We had to perform. For the nation, for the world, pretend that everything was okay when we were...when we were dying."

"What does that have to do with your cuffs?" she asked, her eyes falling to his sleeves. It was one of his many obsessive-looking mannerisms. He straightened his jacket and dress shirt constantly. She had seen him do it frequently from that first meeting.

"There was a state dinner. And my father chose to make that the issue of the day. My jacket sleeve was rolled up, or it was ill fitting, something." A crease appeared between his brows, and there was a measure of confusion in his dark gaze. She had a feeling that he remembered all of it. But that he preferred not to. That he preferred not to show himself and get all of the details right, because the details were so horrifying. "She tried to protect me. She brought me up here. And then my father followed us. And he poured all of his rage out on to her. He struck her. Again, and again. And then she... She went to the window. Then she was gone." He frowned. "I thought about following her. But I thought...I thought it could not be safe. And yet if my mother had just jumped out the window how could it be dangerous?"

His expression went blank. "All of that was answered for me later."

Her throat worked, but she could force no words to her lips.

Felipe regarded her closely. "Have I shocked you?"

She pressed her hand to her breast. "Of course you have. It's a terrible story. It should be shocking. You saw her... You saw your mother..."

"Yes," he said, that same detached tone she had heard from him many times prevalent now. "You can see now why I hate him so much. My father. There was nothing good about him, Briar. Nothing at all."

She nodded silently, swallowing hard.

She looked around the room, surprised that he was standing there. That he was standing so near that window. Had she endured something like that she doubted she would ever have been able to set foot in that room again.

"You're wondering how I'm in here," he said. "It's okay. I understand that it must seem strange to you. That it would seem strange to a great many people. People with a heart. But I cut mine out a long time ago, Briar. Because so long as you care it is dangerous. So long as you care you can be broken. My father tried to break me. He made me come in here. Told me that he would not allow for me to become softer, weak, would not allow me to build a shrine to a dead woman. So I learned." He looked around the space. "There is no real power in this room, anyway.

The real power was in plotting my father's downfall. The real power is in the fact that I now have control of this nation, and that I will right the wrongs that have been perpetuated against the people here. That I will write the history books and I will make sure my father's name is nothing but dirt. These are just four walls and a window. And anyway, the memories are with me wherever I go. I don't have to be here."

For the first time she truly believed he had a monster inside him. One made of memories; one comprised of the past horror he had lived through. And it most certainly drove his actions now. But it wasn't him. It wasn't. All she could do was picture a small boy who had been abandoned. Who had seen something no one should ever see.

Who had thought—naively—that he could perhaps fly out that same window to be with her, because in spite of all the indignity, in spite of all the abuse he had suffered, there was still trust inside him.

Trust that, she had no doubt, had been broken that day.

"You have a heart, Felipe," she said, the words strangled.

He frowned. "I don't. And why would I want one?"

She couldn't answer that. Except, she wanted him to understand that he wasn't broken. That his father didn't have the power to keep him in that blank, emotionless state he had been forced to assume to protect himself. The old man was dead, and he had no power. Not now. She wanted him to know that. Wanted him to understand.

Why? For you? Because you wish it were true?

She took a step back, those thoughts halting her words. Maybe. Maybe it was about her. And about what she wanted him to need from her. She swallowed hard, trying to catch her breath.

She shook her head. "I don't know."

She knew why she wanted him to have one. She wished that she didn't. She wished that she could ignore those thoughts. That she could deny the feelings rushing through her like a wave.

They shouldn't be possible. She should hate him. It shouldn't matter how terrible his childhood was; it shouldn't matter that he was broken, that there was no way he could possibly know how he was supposed to treat another person. He had kidnapped her. Was forcing her into marriage, or as good as forcing her, and she needed to remember that.

The trouble was that she did remember it. All too clearly.

And still…

Still, he made her body tremble. Still, he made her heart ache.

"I know what I need to do. For my country. I don't need a heart to accomplish those things." He closed the distance between them, brushing his knuckles over her cheekbone. "And have I not been kind to you?"

"You kidnapped me."

He waved his hand. "Have I not given you pleasure, *querida*? I believe that I have."

Pleasure isn't love. But she didn't say that. "Yes."

"I don't need a heart for such things. I only need this." He took hold of her hand and pressed it against the front of his slacks, over his hardening arousal.

She couldn't even be angry with him. That was the problem with Felipe.

"You're a very bad man," she said, no censure in her voice. "Do you know that?"

"Yes," he responded flippantly.

Then he kissed her as if to prove that didn't matter, either. And he proved it quite effectively.

Warmth flooded her body, flooded her heart. And there was simply no denying the truth. She loved him. She loved him and it mattered whether or not he had a heart because she needed him to have one so he could love her, too.

Later she might try and figure out if all of this was crazy. Might try and figure out why she felt this way. Right now she just clung to him. And felt a kind of certainty she had never experienced before. She didn't feel different. She didn't feel wrong. Like a misshapen piece shoved into the only available space.

But she wanted—so very much—to be all he needed, and she hoped that she could be. That she could be enough. That she could be...

This was her place. Here with him. Felipe was king, and in order to rule he would need a heart. Whether he believed it or not.

So she was determined to give it back to him.

CHAPTER TEN

FELIPE HADN'T INTENDED to confess all of that to Briar earlier. There was something about her. Something that got beneath his skin, got beneath his defenses. Well, he imagined it was the same thing that got beneath his pants. And frequently. Nothing to be too concerned about.

Neither were the headlines currently calling into question whether or not he was a sociopath. Considering he had broken with tradition and declined to give his father a funeral.

He didn't know why he would make a show of burying a dictator, and he had said as much to the media. Implications had been made—more than implications—that he was no different than the old man. That his lack of compassion—whether or not his father had deserved it—was indicative of a flaw in him, as well.

He could not be certain that wasn't the case. Nobody could be.

He strode out of the media room, tearing at the lapel mic he had been wearing. He was done giving interviews for the time being.

Another error, and he was damned if he could figure out what the hell was driving him. He'd spent years married to a facade, and he couldn't seem to find it now. He was damaging that which he sought to build with his inability to simply play the part he ought to.

Though he didn't know why he was surprised.

He destroyed. It was what he did. No matter whether he wanted to or not.

He was surprised to see Briar walking toward him, dressed as though she was prepared for an evening out. She was wearing a green silk dress that conformed to her curves, with a hemline that fell well above the knee, showing off those endless legs he was so fond of. Of course, he preferred it when they were wrapped around him.

He had half a mind to grab her and drag her to his room now. Whatever plans she had. She was his, after all. His queen. To do with as he pleased. If he wanted her, then she would have to cancel her plans and see to him. He paused, frowning. He wondered if that was the sort of thing his father thought about his mother. About anyone in his life. They were his. His to use as he pleased.

"I was looking for you," she said, her bright smile at odds with the thoughts currently chasing around his head.

"Were you?"

"Yes. I thought we might go out for dinner."

"If you haven't seen the headlines today I have created something of a scandal. Perhaps it would be best if we stayed in."

She looked stubborn. Mutinous. She was quite difficult to argue within that state, he had learned. "I have seen the headlines. People are calling your character into question, and it isn't fair. Of course you shouldn't have thrown a large public funeral for your father. It would have been a farce. I understand that. And that's the entire point of the two of us going out. You want me because you needed my help in softening your image. Well, let me do that."

"I'm not sure I understand."

"We will ostentatiously make an appearance together going for dinner. The entire nation will see that whatever the press says I'm on your side. Whatever anyone says, I stand with you."

Her words rang with the kind of conviction he didn't deserve.

"I'm not certain it will accomplish anything."

Her dark brows lowered. "I am," she said, her tone every inch that of a queen.

"You've grown very comfortable with your new role."

She tossed her head back, her curls bouncing with the movement. "Would you prefer that I remain uncomfortable with it? I think it would be much more effective for both of us if I were comfortable. And I think it would be best for you if you complied with my plan."

"Answer me this, my queen. Are you kidnapping me?"

A smile curved her lips. "Yes."

"Then I suppose I have no option but to comply."

The press was waiting outside the gates to the palace, and when the limousine he and Briar were riding in exited the gates they were nearly mobbed. Briar held on tightly to his arm, glaring out the window. "I would have us present a united front," she said, her tone stiff. "Because I believe that what you did was right. You did it for you, and for your mother. And whether or not anyone else ever understands the full circumstances... I do."

Those simple words caused a strange shift in his chest, and he didn't pause to examine them. Her soft fingertips were drifting down past his arm, over his thigh.

"Careful," he said, his tone full of warning. "The flash photography may make it so they can get shots through the window."

He didn't know how effective the tinted glass would be against those high-powered bulbs.

"I don't care," she said. "Like I said. Let them see that I stand with you. That you're mine.

"I'm going to have the car drop us off a little way from our destination." She tapped on the glass, and the driver lowered the divider. "Leave us just near the university," she commanded.

He quite liked seeing her like this. So at ease with her position. So perfectly at ease in his life. It made him feel much less like questioning himself. Much less like he might be the villain, as he was worried he might have been a few moments earlier.

"There are no restaurants over by the university," he said, reaching out and brushing some of her hair from her face. "Unless you intend to have us eat fast food."

"I'm not opposed to a French fry, Felipe. But that isn't what I have in mind for us tonight. I have a plan. But we need to make sure we're seen a little bit more before we get down to it."

He wrapped his arm around her, burying his face in her hair, his lips touching the shell of her ear. "I'm more than happy to get down to it. We don't even need to have dinner."

"Later," she said, her dark eyes burning with promise. "I promise later."

For some reason, those words caught hold of something in his chest. Sparked a memory. A feeling. One of loss. The kind of loss he hadn't truly allowed himself to feel since he was seven years old.

He caught hold of her chin, held her face steady. "Is that a promise? A real promise? One you won't break."

"Have I ever denied you my body?"

She had not. And still, he couldn't quite credit why that was. "No."

"Then trust me."

He couldn't remember the last time someone had asked him to trust them. Moreover, he couldn't remember the last time he had actually trusted someone. He wanted to. He found that he very much wanted to.

"I will hold that in reserve," he said finally.

The car pulled up to the university, and he and Briar got out, Briar taking hold of his hand as though it was the most natural thing on earth. He couldn't remember the last time anyone had asked him to trust them, and he couldn't remember the last time he had held a woman's hand, either. Had he ever? He had lovers from time to time, fairly frequently, in truth. But their interaction was confined to the bedroom. That meant there was no reason for them to ever walk around with their fingers laced together.

This touch was not... Well, it wasn't sexual. And in his life that meant it was pointless. Except it didn't feel pointless. It felt very much like something essential. Felt very much like air. He couldn't explain it even if he wanted to. He found he didn't. He found he just wanted to enjoy the feeling of her soft skin against his.

It only took him a moment to realize she was taking him to the museum.

"Are you subjecting me to a gala?" He looked at her sideways. "Because I must warn you I am not in the temperament required for a gala."

She narrowed her eyes. "What temperament is required for a gala?"

"Something much more docile than I'm capable of."

She made a dismissive sound. "You don't need to be docile." She tugged on his hand, drawing him toward the entrance. "Of course, this is our own private gala. And our own private dinner."

"I thought the point of coming out was to be seen?"

She pushed open the museum door. "It is. Well, it was. But we were seen as much as I intend for us to be tonight."

She looked at him, her expression slightly mischievous. It made his heart beat faster, made his groin tighten. She grabbed hold of the door and pulled it shut, and impish grin tugging at the corners of her mouth.

"If I didn't know any better I would say you had lured me here to seduce me," he said. He disliked his own tone. It was far too dry, far too insincere, when there was absolutely nothing insincere about Briar. Or this act. He closed some of the distance between them, pressing his hand to her cheek. "That was not a complaint, mind you."

She lifted her own hand, covered his with it. "I didn't take it as one."

"You set dinner out for us?" he asked, doing his best to keep himself from poking at her. From twisting the conversation into something overly light and familiar.

"Well, people who work for you set dinner out for us. I don't know how to cook." She cleared her throat. "But I didn't bring you here to try and impress you with the food."

She turned the lights on, and the entire antechamber lit up, the antique chandelier that hung in the entry blazing into glory. Everything was clean. A statue placed just at the foot of the staircase well lit, showcasing the marble, and the incredible skill of the artist.

"It's nearly ready," she said, nearly bursting with excitement. "I wanted you to see this. I wanted you to see what you have made it possible for your people to have." She turned a circle, her arms spread wide. "All of this history. All of this beauty. It's part of the fabric of this country and it's been hidden from them for so long. But now it won't be. Now everyone can come and see this. Everyone can experience this."

He was humbled. Not so much by the art, not even by the work she had put in here. But by her exuberance for it. The happiness that she felt. Why should she be happy? Why should she be happy here with him? And excited for this task he had assigned to her as something she should be grateful for when he had uprooted her from her home? He didn't understand it. He didn't understand her.

And he didn't understand the kind of unfettered joy she seemed to radiate.

Moreover, he didn't understand the passion that she had for art. For something that seemed to exist for no other reason other than to be beautiful. For no other reason than to be looked at. It was a frivolous beauty, and he had never found much beauty in life at all. But she seemed to relish it. Seemed to worship it almost.

He wondered what it must be like to care like that. To feel like that. To live for something beyond the grim march to a goal.

"Come this way," she said. "They've set a table for us in my favorite wing."

"What is your favorite wing?" he asked, finding that he was unable to wait for the answer to that question to be revealed naturally.

She paused. "Impressionists." She smiled, her expression pretty, clearly pleased with the fact that he had asked.

"Why?" he persisted as he followed her down a long corridor, and into a large, open showroom with paintings mounted on each wall. A table was set in the middle with plates covered by trays. There were no candles, and he found that didn't surprise him.

She wouldn't expose her beloved art to anything that might burn it.

She was clearly puzzled by his question. "I don't know. I mean, I do know. But it's hard to put into words. It speaks to my soul in a way that…resonates beyond language."

Those words put him in the mind of something that resonated in him. It brought to mind images of his hands on her skin. The contrast of his fingers gliding over her dark beauty, an erotic kick to the gut that shocked him every time. The feel of her…of being over her, in her… there was nothing on earth like it.

He'd had sex more times than he could count, with more women than he cared to count. This reached beyond that. He imagined she would not enjoy him comparing their physical relationship to the art she loved so much. But he had no other frame of reference.

"It's not as detailed as some styles," she continued. "It's not perfect. There's something almost…messy about it when you look up close. Chaotic. And yet, when you stand back and you look at the whole picture it creates something beautiful."

"Why does that appeal to you so? You seem like nothing more than perfection to me, Princess."

She tilted her head to the side, her expression full of speculation. "I suppose it's because I like to think that…

if someday I should ever become…something other than what I have tried to be, then somebody would look at me and try to see the beauty. That somebody would step back and see who I am as a whole. And find me lovely."

"You could never be anything less than beautiful," he said, his voice rough. "It would be impossible."

"You're talking about physical appearance. And it isn't that I don't appreciate that," she said, looking down. "It's just that… That isn't all there is. And it isn't really my primary concern. But I always felt that…my parents—the parents I was raised with, not the king and queen—were older when they took me in. And they loved me. They have always behaved as though I was their own. But they never had any children before me. I was the first. And I could tell that though I brought them joy I brought them an equal measure of anxiety. And I did my very best to transcend that. To make up for it. To be worth the sacrifice. Because before I came into their lives they had so much less responsibility. So much less worry. I always felt like I had to do something to offset that. To be the girl that was worth that sacrifice."

"That is quite the feat. For a young girl to attempt to be perfect. To try and justify your existence. A child should never have to do that." His existence had always had purpose, for he was his father's heir. And then in end, his purpose—no matter that it had been a secret one—had been to right the wrongs his father had committed against his people.

But she had wondered. Had wondered what she should do to make herself worthwhile, when she should have known all along she had a kingdom depending on her. When she should have known she had parents in the US and in Verloren who cared for her.

She had not. It had all been hidden from her.

He despised his role in that. The role his family had played in that. His father. But then, that was nothing new. His father ruining lives. Him ruining lives.

"I can't remember any different," she said, her tone soft. "It has always been that way for me. For as long as I can remember."

"Except, you *can* imagine different. If not, you wouldn't like these paintings quite so much."

"Perhaps not."

She stopped talking then, directing him toward the table that was set for two, any staff who might have placed the settings now conspicuously absent.

"If I didn't know any better I would think you were trying to seduce me," he said.

She smiled, her earlier sadness vanishing. "I am," she said, her tone light, cheerful, as she picked up a glass of wine and lifted it to her lips.

"You should know that you don't need to go to so much effort. In fact, you don't need to go to any effort at all. Showing up is about all it takes."

Her expression changed, and suddenly, she looked slightly wistful. "Is that true of me? Or is it true of all women that you…that you do this with?"

"I have never done this with another woman. Oh, of course I have had lovers, Briar. But I have never…I have never *associated* with a woman outside the bedroom."

"Never?"

He shrugged. "You have never had a relationship, either. Why is it so alarming that I haven't?"

"Well, I had never had a sexual relationship with anyone, either. It seems like one should…lead to the other. So yes, *alarming* is the word I would use. That you've been physically intimate with someone and never…"

"You use the word *intimate* to describe sex often, but to me seeking physical release with someone was nothing." He could see by her expression that those words had hurt her. "In the past," he said, softening his tone, not quite sure why he felt the impulse to do so, only knowing that he did not like that he had been responsible for putting that desolate expression on her beautiful face.

"So I'm different?" She sounded so hopeful, and he wondered why on earth she would waste her hope on him.

"It is so important to you to be different." Suddenly the words that she had spoken when they had walked in and spoken of the Impressionists clicked together with these. And he understood. More than that, he cared. Whatever that meant.

"It is not so unusual that a woman would want to be special to her lover." She slid her wineglass back and forth, her focus on the dark liquid.

"Yes, but that is the thing." He pressed his hand over hers, stopping the nervous movement. "You are more than my lover. You are to be my wife. You have more power, more position, in my life than any woman ever has."

She smiled, clearly pleased by that. And he was happy that he had made her smile. He couldn't recall ever taking such pleasure in someone else's happiness before. Except… Dimly, in the recesses of his mind he could remember trying to make his mother happy when his father had just been being an ogre. Could remember trying to make her smile in spite of the abuses they had both suffered.

As if the antics of a little boy could heal the actions of a madman.

They hadn't. Clearly. If they could have, his mother would still be here. She wouldn't have leaped out a window rather than continue to suffer at the hands of his father. Rather than continue to try to deal with a little boy who would always make that situation untenable. Order. His father had wanted order and he hadn't been able to give her that much. Hadn't realized that if he'd simply…

He tugged on his cuffs.

No, he had never been enough. Not when it counted.

Much like then, that smile on Briar's face probably didn't extend as far down as it needed to go. Much like then, he imagined he would be found wanting. But Briar would be queen. And she would have her art. She would have this place. And they had their passion. He would be faithful to her. He remembered then that he had never told her so.

"I will not repeat the sins of my father," he said.

"Which sins?"

"I will be faithful to you."

She blinked. "I didn't realize that was ever up for debate," she said.

"I had not promised you fidelity."

She frowned. "I thought that was a given with marriage. Unless you're an awful person. Like your father."

"I kidnapped you," he said simply. "At what point did you begin thinking I was a decent man?"

"You've never hurt me. I understand why you did what you did," she said, looking down at where his hand was still pressed over the top of hers. "I understand why you need my help. And I'm honestly happy to give it."

Suddenly, he didn't like that. Didn't like that she was offering him help. That she was putting herself forward as another mark of her perfection. He didn't want that.

Perversely, he wanted her to be with him because she wanted to be.

There was no logic in that. To want that from the woman he had forced to accept his proposal.

Offer her freedom. See what she does.

No. He could not do that. She couldn't have her freedom. She could not be given that opportunity. Because he needed her. He did. Whatever he wanted, he would have to be content with what they had.

There was no reason he should not be. He had everything he wanted.

He would not be everything she wanted, that was inescapable. For this was not the life she had chosen for herself. And why did he care about that at all? Only a few weeks ago he would not have. He had not. He had kidnapped her from a hospital for God's sake.

And now, sitting here in this quiet museum with her, his hand pressed over the top of her knuckles, he burned. Ached. Wanted more than he should. Wanted things that conflicted with his goals.

"If you're offering martyrdom to me—the kind of martyrdom that you gave your parents—then I will state for the record that I don't want it."

"You want me to help with your cause. To comply with your wishes. You never cared why I was giving it before. You threatened me, in fact, if I didn't give it. How can it not be martyrdom?"

"You're offering me your help, saying that you understand, looking at me with those angelic eyes of yours… Pity. You look at me like I'm a dog you *pity*. I may have taken that from my queen, but not from my lover."

"I'm trying to help. I'm trying to do what's expected of me. I'm trying to find my place here. This is for me as much as it is for you. I never knew where I fit. All my life I didn't know. I felt wrong. I knew I had come from somewhere else. I knew that. There were people all around me who can trace their lineage back to the Mayflower and I couldn't trace mine back to my parents. I couldn't remember the first four years of my life. Well, apparently, I was born to be royalty. So here I am. And I'm trying my very best. To make this mine. To make a place for myself. And you're accusing me of playing at empty perfection."

He didn't know why he was pressing this. Didn't know why he cared at all. Mostly, he didn't know why there was a howling, wrenching pain in his chest when he thought of her simply lying back and doing her duty for him.

He wanted to mess her up. Mess them both up.

"I have pushed you every step of the way," he said. "And you... You seem completely and utterly compelled to prove your worth. Why should I think it's anything different?"

She stood, pushing her chair back, her dark gaze level with his. "What do you need? You need some sort of symbol that I'm here on my own? That I'm making choices? That this isn't about me simply complying quietly?"

She reached behind her back, and he heard the soft sound of a zipper. Then she stepped out of her dress. The shimmering fabric fell to her hips, and she pushed it down all the way to the floor.

"When have I ever complied quietly when it comes to you, Felipe?" She unhooked her bra, pushed it down her arms and then sent her panties along the same path, until she was standing naked before him wearing nothing more than a pair of high heels that made her impossibly long legs seem all that much longer. "I screamed and shouted at you as you kidnapped me from the hospital. I refused you until…"

"Perhaps only until you found that there was enough here to make compliance worth it." He was pushing. Pushing hard. And he wanted to see how hard she would push back.

She moved to him, and he stayed seated in his chair, allowed her to curl her fingers around the back of it, to lean over him, her breasts hovering temptingly close to his lips. "Do you think I'm weak? Do you think I'm frightened of you?"

"I think you should be." He lifted his hand and touched her chin. "I ruin people." Then he tilted his face up and scraped his teeth along the underside of her chin. "If you think that by playing perfect you can somehow outrun that fate, then I have news for you."

"Perhaps you should ruin me. Perhaps…we all need to be a little bit ruined. Like one of my paintings."

It so closely echoed his earlier thoughts that it blanked his mind for a moment. But she seemed to be able to read him. That she seemed to…understand him. And that she had not run in the other direction.

He placed his hands on her shoulder blades then slid his fingertips down the elegant line of her spine, to the perfect curve of her ass. He was already so hard he hurt, his arousal pressing against the front of his slacks.

He reached up then, forking his fingers in her hair, curling his fingers around the massive curls and tugging her head back as he pulled her more firmly onto his lap, rolling his hips upward, well aware that he was rubbing his hardness against that place she was already wet and needy for him. She was undoing him, he couldn't deny it. But he would see her undone, as well.

If he was going to break, she would break along with him. They would break together.

He leaned forward, pressing a kiss to the pounding pulse at the base of her neck, then tracing a trail up to her jaw with the tip of his tongue, along upward to her lips, where he claimed her fiercely, with no delicacy at all.

She gasped, her fingers working clumsily on the front of his shirt, tearing at his tie, at the buttons there. And then she gave up, hands moving to his belt buckle, tugging at the fabric until she freed his erection. She curled her delicate fingers around him, her hand small and dark, soft, over that rock-hard arousal, the contrast an aphrodisiac that nearly sent him over the edge.

"Show me," he said, planting his hands on her hips, holding her steady over him. "Show me how much you want me."

Keeping her hand on him, she tilted her hips forward and guided him toward her slick entrance, placing him there, slowly lowering herself onto him. His breath hissed through his teeth and he let his head fall back, let himself get lost in all that tight, glorious heat.

It was tempting to close his eyes, to shut everything out except for that sensation. But he forced himself to keep them open, so that he could look at her. So that he could watch the glorious bounce of her breasts as she rocked herself up and down over him.

He looked beyond her shoulders, at all the art that was mounted on the walls. She rivaled all of it. Made these masterworks as finger paintings in his eyes. He slipped his hands up to her narrow waist, holding her hard as she moved.

Then he leaned forward, capturing one of her nipples with his mouth, sucking it in deep. She let out a low, hoarse sound and her pleasure exploded all around him. She didn't close her eyes; instead, she looked deep into his, her expression one of fierce intensity and concentration.

This was just for him. She had never even kissed another man before him. She had certainly never come for another man. And here he was, buried deep inside her, wringing out every last bit of her pleasure, taking it on as his own. He didn't deserve it. Didn't deserve her. And yet, he couldn't stop. Couldn't fathom not taking this. Not taking her.

She tossed her head back at the last moment, planting her hands on his shoulders as she ground her hips against his, extracting each and every possible wave of pleasure from him, her climax a fierce and wild thing he didn't deserve in the least.

When she righted herself, when she looked at him again, he was the one who had to look away. He was undone by that emotion in her eyes. A vulnerability that ran beneath the strength he had just seen. The kind of vulnerability a man like him could exploit. A softness he could so easily destroy.

The sort of thing he would do well to be gentle with. And yet he found himself tightening his hold on her. Driving himself up inside her as he chased his own release. As he allowed that white-hot wave to wash over him, to steal every thought, every doubt, from his mind. At the moment he was inside Briar. And she was all around him. Her soft skin, her delicate scent, everything that she was filling him, consuming him.

A soft smile curved her lips, an expression of wonder on her face. She cupped his head in her hands, sliding her thumbs along the line of his jaw as she gazed down at him. No one had ever looked at him like this before. As if he were a thing they had never before seen. As if he were something magic.

He should explain to her that he was not magic. He was not unique. And he would only destroy her.

Instead, he found himself reaching up, wrapping his hands around her wrists, pulling her more firmly against him, forcing her to wrap her arms around his neck. His lips pressed against hers, and when he spoke it was nearly a growl. "We will be married next week. Then you will truly be mine."

Her lashes fluttered, a slight hint of shock visible in those dark eyes. But then she smiled. "I'm glad."

She shouldn't be. And he had a feeling in time she wouldn't be. But self-sacrifice was for another man, a better man. And if he was a man capable of those things, perhaps he would be worthy of her.

And so it was an impossible situation. For *her.*

As for him, he would have what he wanted.

The dragon inside him was content. And the man… Well, the man wanted her already, all over again. As though she had opened up a need inside him that he'd never before known existed. One he was afraid would never entirely be satisfied again.

Good thing they would have a lifetime for him to try and exhaust it.

Then she did something he could not have anticipated. She leaned forward, kissing him softly, sweetly. And then she spoke.

"I love you."

CHAPTER ELEVEN

SHE HADN'T INTENDED to say that out loud. But now that she had she couldn't regret it. Wouldn't regret it. How could she? She had fallen in love, for the first time in her life. With this wild, untamable man who had suffered unimaginable loss. Who had endured unimaginable pain. And she just wanted to give to him. She wanted him to feel everything that she did. This bright, intense emotion in her chest that made it difficult for her to breathe, that made her want to cry and laugh and shout all at the same time.

She felt brave, and she felt frightened. She felt more than she had ever felt in her life. And she felt everything. How could she not share it?

"I wasn't looking for that," he said, his voice flat. Hands planted on her hips, he removed her from his lap, and she felt the loss of him keenly, leaving her body and her heart feeling cold. She wrapped her arms around herself, raised goose bumps covering her arms.

"That's all right. I offered it anyway."

"Why? Because it makes you feel better about accepting my proposal? Make no mistake, Princess. It is not a proposal, but a demand. You do not have to offer anything in return. Unless it's simply to salve your own conscience." He narrowed his dark eyes. "Is that the issue? You're disturbed by the fact that you enjoy the body of a man you don't love? So you had to manufacture emotions in order to justify your orgasm?"

Heat seared her cheeks, wiping out the cold sensation that had rocked her only moments earlier. "I don't feel the need to justify any orgasm I've had with you," she said, not quite sure where her boldness was coming from. "I wanted you, and I was never ashamed of that, regardless of the emotions involved. I had never wanted a man before, and I can't think of a better reason to be with someone and wanting them the way that I wanted you. That isn't why I love you."

A cold, cruel smile quirked the side of his mouth. "Go on, then. Enumerate the reasons you find me emotionally irresistible. I can provide you with several reasons why you find me physically irresistible, as I'm not a modest man, neither am I unaware of the charms that I present to women. So if any of it has to do with my body I shall have to sadly inform you that your reasoning is neither original nor rooted in finer feelings. That is lust, my darling, and nothing more."

She recognized this. This kind of bitter banter that played at being light but was designed to cut and wound, was designed to keep the target at a distance. He had done it from the beginning, and only recently had he made an effort to connect with her in ways that went deeper than this. But he was retreating.

He was also misjudging her. Sadly for him, she did know him. More than just his body, and she saw this for exactly what it was.

She wanted to fix it. Wanted to find a way to be what he needed. To be…

She wanted so much to keep him. To have his heart and not just his body. To be the wife he didn't know he wanted.

She wanted to be perfect for him.

"You are strong," she said. "Determined. You believe in doing what's right, even if you have to do the wrong things to accomplish it. Your moral code might not be the same as what the rest of the world would call good, but you have one. And it is strong."

He laughed. "Yes. So very strong. In that I do everything within my power to establish myself as a better ruler than my father, to ensure that my place in the history books is superior to his. To create a country richer in resources and wealth, to forge better alliances with neighboring nations. If you imagine me to be altruistic, I will have to disappoint you on that score. I'm simply much less base than my father was, much smarter about how I might wield my power."

"It suits you to say that, and I can guess at why that might be. But that isn't the beginning and end of it. I know it, whether you do or not."

"You suppose that you know my motivations better than I do?"

"Yes. Because I think you're hiding from your motivations. I think you hide from a great many things, and I can't blame you. You were forced into hiding as a child because of the way that your father treated you."

He laughed, hard and flat. "Oh, no, Princess, do not make the mistake of imagining that I am some little boy trapped inside a man's body, still cowering in fear. That little boy was obliterated long ago. I did learn how to survive, and it was by hardening myself. I might not have thrown myself out the window that day, but my mother took a piece of me with her, and I gladly surrendered it. Love. I am not capable of it, not anymore. And I don't want to be. So whatever you say, whatever you feel you must force yourself to feel for me… Understand that I cannot return it. I will gladly take your body, Briar, for I am not a good man, and I'm not a soft man. All that I can give you in return is pleasure."

Once again, she found herself standing before him naked while he was clothed. Vulnerable while he seemed impenetrable. But she knew that wasn't the case. Knew that it was all an illusion. She was naked because she was strong. It takes a great amount of strength to stand before somebody without any covering, not on her body, not on her soul.

He, on the other hand, was desperately concealing all that he was. Was trying so hard to protect himself with that barrier that he had placed between them. And she could understand it in a great many ways. Sometimes she wondered if she had held herself apart from friends, from men, if she had set about to working so hard on this idea of perfection and earning her place because she was afraid of loss. Because even though she couldn't remember her life before going to live with her parents in New York, that feeling, that emptiness, lived inside her. A memory that didn't reside in her brain, but in her heart.

"I don't believe that," she said, her tone muted. "I don't believe that it's all you have inside you. Maybe it's all you feel you can give right now, but I don't think it's all we'll have forever. And I can wait. I can wait until you love me."

"I won't," he said, the words clipped, hard. "I cannot."

Her throat tightened, tears stinging her eyes. "Then I suppose I'll have to love you enough for both of us."

"You're still going to marry me?"

She nodded. "Of course I am. We didn't start here because of love. Why should it end because of a lack of it?"

It was easy to say, but she felt…devastated. A part of her destroyed that she would have said didn't exist. Because how could she hope for Felipe to love her? How had they gotten here? It still mystified her in some ways.

That she had gone from being terrified of him, from hating him, to needing him more than she needed her next breath. But he was… He was the most extraordinary man. So strong. And most definitely not loved enough.

Right then she felt a surge of anger—not at his father, but at his mother. For leaving him. How dared she? Why couldn't she have stayed for him? Shouldn't love have been enough to make her stay and protect that little boy? Or try to find a way to escape, but with him?

She would stay. No matter what he said he could give. Because she did believe that in the end he would find more for her. That they would have more. No one had stayed for him; no one had ever truly demonstrated their love for him. Well, she would be the first one. Even if it hurt.

She would be what he needed, because it was what she needed.

"Very pragmatic," he said, his tone as opaque as his expression.

"It's not, actually," she said. "It's just… Perhaps a bit blindly hopeful. But I feel like one of us needs to be, Felipe. You want your country to have beauty. You want it to be filled with the kind of light it's been missing… Well, I think one of us needs to believe in it in order for that to be accomplished, don't you?"

He reached out, gripping the back of her neck, drawing her to him, kissing her fiercely. "You're welcome to hope for that, Briar. You're welcome to believe in it. But don't be surprised when all you're met with is darkness."

She had difficulty talking to Felipe over the next few days. But at night he remained as passionate as ever. He announced the wedding to the media that very next day, and Briar's head was spinning with how quickly an elaborate event could come together when you had unlimited wealth and power.

She had a wedding dress fitted to her in record time, the design altered so that it was unique only to her. A menu had been planned, elaborate cakes conceptualized. Somehow, a massive guest list had been amassed, with RSVPs coming in fast. If anyone had something else to do, they had certainly rearranged their schedules quickly enough.

The wedding of Prince Felipe Carrión de la Viña Cortez to the long-lost Princess Talia was definitely a worldwide curiosity. The kind of event that everyone wanted to be included in.

For her part, Briar felt numb. Her parents—both sets— had been invited to the wedding and she felt strange and had trepidations about seeing both of them. Mostly because she had a feeling they would all try to talk her into calling it off. Even though everyone involved knew that was something that couldn't be afforded. Plus, at this point, she didn't want it called off.

Regardless of what he had said to her the other day, she still loved him. In fact, watching him put this wedding together, watching him contend with matters of the state, with his new position, only made her love him more.

The morning of the wedding dawned bright and clear,

the preparations being made about the palace awe-inspiring as far as Briar was concerned. But she didn't have a chance to observe the decorating process to the degree that she wanted to, because she was accosted by her stylists early in the day and subjected to a beauty regimen that left her feeling like she had run a marathon.

She was scraped, scrubbed, plucked and waxed, left so that she was glowing to an almost supernatural degree. Her hair was tamed into an elaborate up-do, some kind of powder that left her glowing brushed over her face, her lips done in a deep cherry color, her fingernails painted to match.

Large gold earrings with matching gems weighed down her ears, and a crown was placed on top of her head, heavy and unfamiliar.

The gown had a fitted bodice, the skirt voluminous, great folds of white, heavy satin fashioned into pleats, falling all the way to the ground, and trailing behind her in a dramatic train.

She had to admit, she certainly looked like a princess bride. She only hoped that she would be the bride of Felipe's dreams. She clasped her hands in front of her, twisting her fingers. Maybe she was foolish; he certainly thought that she was. To hope that this could ever be more than a bloodless transaction, necessary for him to gain the sort of reputation in the world that he coveted.

But she had to believe it. Someone had to believe in them. Believe in him. She did. And she would do it until... Until he left her no other choice.

She was supposed to marry him, after all. For better or worse. Until death did them part.

Nerves twisted low in her belly and she pressed her

palm up against herself, taking a long, slow breath out, hoping that she would find some sense of calm. Of peace.

Then the door to her bedchamber opened, and her eyes clashed with Felipe's. There was no calm to be had there. Just a sort of dark excitement that hit her all at once like a freight train. There was nothing that could prepare her for the impact, not even after weeks of being his lover.

She wondered if he would ever become common-place, this man who had the face of a fallen angel and the body of a Greek god, and a soul that had every dark thing imaginable crammed into it, until that gorgeous, mortal frame—for however perfectly he was formed, he was mortal—seemed as though it might crack from the force of it.

How could a man such as that ever be common? How could he ever fail to make her feel things? Everything.

How could she ever give up on him? It was inconceivable. Unfathomable.

"You're not supposed to see me before the wedding," she said.

He laughed, flinging himself down onto an armchair. "Because the beginning of our relationship was so auspicious and traditional you're going to concern yourself with superstition now?"

She lifted a bare shoulder. "I suppose at this point we are somewhat bulletproof."

His expression turned dark. "Nothing is. Are you prepared for this?"

"I don't know. Can anyone really prepare for something they've never done before? Lifelong commitment and all of that."

"And if you marry me," he said, his tone uncompromising, "it will be a lifelong commitment."

She couldn't quite place the thread running underneath those words, hard and angry-sounding though they were. There was something else. But with Felipe there was always something else. There had been from the first moment she had met him. He covered it all up with that world-weary cynicism of his, with that brittle banter designed to make the recipient die of a thousand small cuts.

But there was more. He was just so very desperate to hide it. She wanted to uncover it. But that probably would be bad luck before their wedding. If she did that, he could well and truly crack. Spilling all the dark things out into the room. She wasn't afraid of that. She knew the day would come eventually.

She just thought that maybe…just maybe…it wouldn't happen right before they took their vows. Anyway, while she wasn't afraid of it, she had a feeling that he might be.

"I know that, Felipe. If you recall, I love you, so it isn't really going to be a great burden for me to bind myself to you for the rest of my life. Actually, when you love someone you consider that something of a goal."

He flinched when she spoke those words, as though she had struck him. "So you say," he responded.

"Did you want me to throw myself on the ground and scream about how I shan't marry you, because you're a brute and I cannot possibly fathom a future with you? It would be both embarrassing and disingenuous. Plus, I would mess up my hair."

"It would make more sense than this," he said, standing, waving his arm at her standing there in her wedding gown. "You are far too serene. Far too accepting of your fate."

"You say fate, I say destiny."

"They end in the same place, Princess," he said, his

tone brittle. "Either way, I expected a bit more in the way of hysterics on this day of days."

"Why? Haven't I demonstrated to you over the past weeks that I'm here with you? You threw everyone out of that ballroom, Felipe. You told everyone to leave, and yet I remained. You told me about your mother, we stood together. I showed you my artwork. I gave you my body. I have continued to do so every night in the days since, and I will do it every night after. You're the only one who seems to be perturbed by the impending wedding. The one that you literally crossed the world and committed a crime to make happen."

He scowled, his dark mood rolling off him in waves. "I am not. What surprises me is your lack of emotion." He prowled across the room, stopping in front of her. "You should feel something. You should do something."

"I professed my love. It's really not my fault you don't acknowledge that as an emotion, Felipe. But there are other emotions beyond rage. Beyond grief. Beyond hatred. They are no less valid."

"Yes, you seem overjoyed."

She blinked, the corners of her lips tugging down. "I'm not sure that I am overjoyed," she said honestly. "I'm slightly afraid. Of how it will be between us. Of what might happen along the way. Of the ways in which you might hurt me. But I love you. And I've made my decision. I'm not going to pretend. I'm not going to paste a smile onto my face when my feelings are more complicated than that."

That seemed to light a match on the gasoline of his anger. "So you admit you are not thrilled to marry me. All your posturing about love and forever was simply that. Why don't you fight against it? Why don't you do something other than stand there grimly prepared to do your duty? Lying to both of us about how you feel so you can try to justify what's about to occur? Why do you have to be so damned perfect all the time?" He wrapped his arm around her waist, pulling her hard against his chest.

"I'm not," she said, her voice strangled. "I'm not. And I don't know what I have to do to show you that that isn't what this is. Stripping naked in a museum wasn't enough? Telling you about how hard I worked all that time to earn love… That wasn't enough?"

"No," he said, his voice rough, "it's not enough. You're here because you want access to your family. Because now you're afraid to leave, because you're afraid of the state you believe the nation in. You're a martyr," he said, spitting those words, "and what you do is for your own conscience. So that you can feel important. So you can feel special. And if you have to call it love in order to make yourself feel better then you will. But that's not going to insulate you against a lifetime with me, Princess."

He said those words as though they were intended to push her away, and yet he tightened his hold on her as they escaped his lips. And she was not such a fool.

She reached up, grabbing hold of his tie. "I don't need insulation. Don't you dare accuse me of being weak. Don't you dare accuse me of lying to myself, or to you, about my feelings. I spent my life trying to simply get through and make no waves. Trying to be worthy of the sacrifice my birth parents had made for me, and of the upending of the lives of my parents who raised me. You're right. I did spend my life trying to be perfect. Trying to do the right thing. The best thing. Trying to do my best to make sure nobody regretted taking me on. But that's not what I'm doing with you. I'm not afraid of you. I'm not afraid to fight against you. I'm not afraid to push you. Do not mistake me, King Felipe. When I say I am prepared to stand as your queen it is not so that I can be an accessory to you. Not so I can stand demurely at your side. I intend to make a difference. I intend to make a difference not just in this country but in your life. If I have to push you then I will do so. If I have to fight you, I will do that, too. You will never become your father, Felipe, because I will not allow it. Because I see more in you, and I see bettering you. You might not know it's there, but I do. *I do.*"

He wrapped his fingers around her wrist, pulled her arm back, prying her fingers off his tie. "Do you think my mother thought she would be crushed beneath the boot heel of my father? I highly doubt that was her goal. And yet… And *yet.*"

"I'm not your mother," she said, brushing her fingertips over his lips, satisfied when he jerked beneath the touch. "And you're not your father."

"Such confidence in me," he said, parting his lips, scraping his teeth over her fingers, leaving a slight stinging sensation behind. "For what? And why?"

"Love, Felipe. The very thing you keep dismissing as a lie. As an incidental. It's not. It's everything. It's what will keep you grounded. It's what keeps me here with you. I want to be here with you. I want to be what you need. I want to be perfect for you."

Her words echoed between them, and they made her stomach sink.

It was all so circular.

She had been consumed with being perfect for her mother and father, and then she'd come here and found a freedom in her lack of caring. But now she did care. Now she loved him. And she was back to trying to be whatever she had to be.

She could see the moment he heard it, too. The moment he realized what it meant.

"Was it love that saw my mother jumping from a window, Briar?" he asked, his voice rough. "Because that's the only love I've ever known," he said, his voice rough, harsh. "It's soft and weak. It can be used against you. Used to destroy you."

"You think you'll destroy me, Felipe? And you're angry at me for believing differently? Is that what's happening here?" Nerves ate at her as her own words began to fray. Would he destroy her? He had the power to do so now. Now that she cared.

"Why should you believe in me at all?" he asked, his tone harsh. "There is nothing good in that. Nothing good that could possibly result from it."

"What do you want? You want to drag me kicking and screaming down the aisle so that you can be thought of as a villain by your people? That isn't true, because you care about your reputation. So I can only imagine it's yourself you're playing the villain for. But I can't for the life of me figure out why."

"You're trying to figure me out as if I am a puzzle, *querida*. But you assume there are pieces for you to assemble. I am broken beyond repair. I told you already, my mother took her last leap with my heart, and there is no fixing that. But more important, I don't want it fixed."

"Stop trying to be so damned messed up all the time," she said, shooting his words back at him. "Don't commit yourself to this. You accuse me of being a martyr, but what are you, Felipe? You're determined to atone for your father's sins, but must you punish yourself for them, as well?"

"Someone has to," he said. "The old man is dead, and for all that I hope he's burning in hell, the only assurance I have that things will ever be right is what I fix in this life."

"But you can't have anything good while you work at that?"

"I can't..." He closed his mouth, a muscle working in his jaw. "I cannot afford distraction."

She knew that wasn't what he'd been about to say. That there was something else. But she also knew he wasn't going to let his guard down enough to actually speak with any honesty. There was something about this—whether it was the wedding, the sight of her, or the declaration of love—that unnerved him. That...that scared him. And no matter how deep he might deny it, she could see it.

If she could just make him see. She needed him to see. She had to make him understand that she could be what he needed. That she could fix this. That...

It hit her again, what was happening now.

She had convinced herself that if she behaved in a certain way she could earn his love. Could make him see that she wasn't a burden. That she was everything he needed. That in the end, he would be happier for having her in his life, if she would only just...find the perfect way to be.

She couldn't step back into that. She couldn't do that to herself. Mostly, she could not be the woman he needed her to be if she did. He was so afraid of breaking her. And if she didn't learn how to stand on her own, he might, and it wouldn't even be his fault. She couldn't force him to change. No amount of smiling prettily and inviting him into her bed could do that. He was going to have to love her.

She was going to have to demand that. Not sit around and wait for it.

She was going to have to make waves. There was no other option. She was going to have to take a risk that in the end she wouldn't be worth it. It was the one thing she had always feared most. That ultimately, she would be far too much of an inconvenience for her parents if she stepped out of line. That everyone would find her to be too much trouble to care about. Unless she acted just so. Unless she contributed just enough.

She had stopped. She had to stop or it would go on forever. And it could not.

She took a deep breath and looked up at him, trembling from the inside out. "I love you, Felipe," she said, the words steady.

"So you have said."

"Do you love me?"

"I already gave you my answer."

"I know. But I have to ask again. Because I have to be absolutely certain."

"I cannot," he said, his voice rough. "It is not in me."

She nodded slowly. "I understand. And I need you to understand this. I can't marry you. Not without your love."

"Oh, so suddenly now you require love. Before you said this was never about love, and it wouldn't change."

"Well... I changed."

"What do you want from me? You want me to lie to you, say the words and they will somehow have the magic power to force you to walk down the aisle?"

Her throat started to close up, her hands shaking, misery threatening to overwhelm her. She wanted—with almost everything she had, everything she was—to throw herself on the ground in front of him and tell him she didn't mean it. That she would marry him no matter what. That she would stay with him forever and just hope that everything worked out okay.

And she would grow dimmer and dimmer. And he would consume her. In the end, it would sign both of their death warrants. For their happiness, at least.

"No," she said, forcing the word through her tightened throat. "I would know. If you turned around and said it to me now I would know that you didn't mean it."

"And so you have forced me into an impossible situation."

"You forced us into an impossible situation, Felipe. Because you are not the monster that you seem to think you are, not the monster that you wish you were. You kidnapped me, you dragged me here. And if you had been truly awful it would have been easy for me to resist you. But the fact is you aren't. You're simply broken. And whatever you say, you're more that little boy who lost his mother all those years ago than you are a dragon. But I can't fix it for you. I've tried. And I will break myself in the process. You're right. I can't martyr myself to this cause. You asked me to reconsider. That's what you came here for. To push me away. To make it so that I would leave." She blinked hard, tears threatening to fall. But she wouldn't let them. "Congratulations. You've won."

"There is an entire room full of guests waiting for us to say our vows, Princess. You would disappoint them?"

"I would disappoint them now rather than devastate myself later. It has to be done. I have to go. And if, when I am gone you are able to look inside yourself and find that heart you seem to think doesn't exist… Then you can come and find me."

"And if you leave," he said, his lip curling up into a sneer, "you know that I will make things very difficult for your mother and father."

She nodded slowly; this time a tear did track down her cheek. "I know."

"And you will have failed everyone," he said, the words hard, cruel. "You will have failed me, you will have failed Santa Milagro, you will have failed your adoptive parents, the king and queen, and Verloren herself. Is that what you want?"

She shook her head. "No. It isn't what I want. It's the last thing I want. But sadly, I could never be Princess Talia. I could never be the person I was born to be. I've only ever been able to be Briar Harcourt. She doesn't want any of those things. But she does want to be loved. And at the end of the day, I think she deserves it." She shook her head, battling with the ridiculousness of speaking about herself in the third person. But it was so hard to say what she knew she needed to say. "I deserve to be loved. I deserve it. I don't need to earn it. I shouldn't have to. Someday, Felipe, I'm going to find a man who wants me. One who didn't track me down to the ends of the earth simply because I presented a political advantage to him. But a man who would track me down to the end of the world if I could offer him nothing but a kiss. If I came with no title. If I was only me. I have…I have never been able to say that I thought I deserved such a thing. That I've possessed enough value to be worthy of it. But now I do."

She looked down at the ring, sparkling on her finger. A ring that represented a promise that would now not be fulfilled. She slipped it off, held it out to him. "I suppose I'm the monster now," she said softly, dropping the gem into his open palm. "But I'm a monster that you created. You made me more myself than I have ever been. But I fear that if I stay here it won't last. It will only fade away as I try everything in my power to please you, to make you love me the way that I love you. We both deserve more than that. Because it will only be a self-fulfilling prophecy, don't you see? I will begin to feel I don't deserve love, as I cannot earn it. And you will become the monster you were always afraid you were while you break me slowly into tiny pieces. I won't do that to you. I won't do it to me."

She stood, and she waited. Because whatever she had said if he was to fling himself at her feet, if he was to grab her and pull her into his arms and confess his undying love, she would surely stay. Even if it was a lie. It would take nothing. A half a beat of his heart, a flutter of his eyelash, an upward curve to his lip. Just a sign. A small one, and she would crumble completely, all her good intentions reduced to ash.

"Get out," he said, his voice hard.

"What?"

"You heard me. Get out of my sight. Get out of my palace." He cocked his arm back, threw her ring across the room with a ferocity that shocked her. It was a gem of near inestimable value and he had cast it aside as though it was garbage.

Still, she didn't obey him. She simply stood, shocked, unable to move.

"Get out!" He shouted now then turned to the side and grabbed hold of her vanity, tipping it over onto its face, the glass shattering from the mirror, small bottles of perfume smashing on the tile and sending heavy, drugging scents into the air.

She jumped backward, pressing her palm against her chest, her heart fluttering in her breasts. But still she felt rooted to the spot.

He advanced on her, radiating fury, his eyes a black flame. "Do you think I'm joking? Do you think I am anything less than the product of my father's genetics and upbringing? Do you think I am anything less than a monster? Get out of my sight. Pray that I never see you again, Princess, because if I do I cannot promise you I will not make you my prisoner again. But this time, it will be far less pleasurable for you, I can assure you."

"Felipe…"

He reached out, gripping her chin, the hold hard and nearly painful. "I do not love you. I do not possess the capacity. But oh, how I can hate. You do not want to test the limits of that."

He turned and walked away from her then, and perversely she missed his touch. Even though it had hurt. Because this was worse. This total separation from him. This finality. It was for the best, and she knew it. By doing this she had revealed his true colors. Had uncovered the truth as it was in his heart. If he could not love her to keep her with him, then he never would.

"You had best not be here when I return," he said finally before he walked out the double doors to her room, closing them behind him with a finality that reverberated through her entire frame.

She looked around the room, panic clawing at her. She didn't know what to do, didn't know where to go.

She took a breath and tried to keep calm. She had just done what needed to be done. But she felt terrible. She didn't feel better at all, and she had a feeling it would be a long time before she did. She waited a few moments. Waited until she was certain Felipe wouldn't be standing out there in the hall.

And then she flung the doors open, picked up the front of her dress and ran through the empty corridor. She ran until her lungs burned. Until she reached the front of the palace, going straight out the doors and across the courtyard. There were steps that led up to an exit point that she knew would be less watched, and she tried to scramble up them, taking them two at a time. And then she slipped and fell, her knees hitting the edge of the stones, her dress trailing behind her. She just lay there for a moment, feeling like this was a perfectly fitting moment for how she felt inside.

But then she pushed up, getting back to her feet. Because there was nothing else to be done. She had made the decision. And there was no going back. She had decided that she was worthy of love. No matter what she submitted herself to, or refused to submit herself to. She should be more than payment for her father's debt.

She should be more than Felipe's humanizing face that was presented to the people. More than a perfect daughter.

She was Briar. No matter who she had been born as. That was who she had become. And she needed to keep on becoming that. Because it was ongoing. Because she wasn't finished. And if she stayed here and allowed her desire to please him to become all that she was…

She couldn't. No matter how badly it hurt to leave. She would only hurt them both if she stayed.

CHAPTER TWELVE

FELIPE HAD CERTAINLY created headlines on his wedding day, but they were not the headlines he had hoped they might be. No, rather than photographs of the happy couple, the news media was filled with photographs of him storming into the chapel and demanding everybody leave. A repeat of the night his father had passed away, and proof that he was no more stable than the previous ruler, at least, so said a great many of the papers.

His lungs were burning as he walked up the stairs to the tower. He didn't know why he was going to the tower. One of the things his father had done early on—shortly after his mother had killed herself—was drag Felipe back up to the tower. He had demanded that he stand there. Demanded that he look out the window and see that there was no longer anything there.

"There is nothing," his father had said. "No ghosts. No bodies. She is gone. And she isn't coming back. This place holds no power. Emotion has no place here. And it certainly shouldn't sway you as a ruler."

Felipe laughed cynically as he remembered that. Of course his father would say that emotion had no power. But he didn't mean anger. He didn't mean rage.

It struck him then, with clarity—a disturbing clarity—that he held a similar worldview. That love didn't count. That happiness was something that could easily be destroyed. Those were the emotions he had banished from himself. All while retaining the kind of toxicity his father had carried around with him.

He walked across the room, making his way over to the window. He wrapped his fingers around the bars. Briar had left him, and it was for the best that she had done so by going out the front door and not flinging herself from a tower.

He also despised that she had taken his words and thrown them back at him. That she had done exactly what he had been trying to get her to do. He had wanted her to leave, in the end. But he had thought that...

Perversely, he had hoped that in the end that love, that he felt was such a folly, that he considered a weakness, would prove to be the thing that was strong enough to hold her to him. It was wrong, particularly when his aim had been to get her to call the wedding off, and yet, part of him had hoped.

He had goaded her. He had pushed her. And in the end she had made the right decision; he knew it because he didn't possess the kind of softness in him that she deserved. He knew only how to break things. How to break people.

Pushing his hand through the bars, he rested his palm on the window. "I am sorry, Mama. I truly am." And then he pounded his fist against the glass, watching it crack, splinters embedding in his skin. He relished that pain. As he had done earlier. As he had done for a great many years. Punishing himself because his father was no longer able to do it.

And, oh, how he loved to break things. Because the old man wanted order. And Felipe wanted to defy that.

And then you straighten your shirtsleeves like a naughty boy.

He pounded his forehead with his bleeding fist then lowered his hand slowly, his heart threatening to rage right out of his chest.

For the first time he wondered if he was not like his father. He wondered if he was merely controlled by him. If he had allowed the old man to gain access to him. No. He was going to make his country better. He was going to atone.

And yet you let him steal your ability to love, with all that fear he gave you. You let him cost you Briar.

He gritted his teeth. No, letting Briar go had been a kindness. Because as she had said to him it would only damage them both in the end if the two of them were to be together.

He thought of her, of everything she had told him about the way she had grown up. So afraid that she would be found unworthy. So desperate to prove her value.

All she had to do for him was simply breathe.

The thought of her… Well, it created a pain in his chest that was so severe it blotted out the pain in his hand.

What was it? All of this pain. He wasn't supposed to be able to feel anything. He had made sure. He had promised himself.

He curled his fingers around the window bars again.

He had promised her.

He hadn't been brave enough to follow her. And so he had done what he thought was best. He had sent the most vital part of himself with her. Had consigned it to the grave. Because he had failed her. In the end, it had been his fault.

He clutched his chest, unable to breathe. His heart. His *heart*. Of course, he knew that his heart was there physically. It was the metaphorical heart he had long since surrendered. But if so then why did it hurt so badly now? Why did it feel as though he was going to suffer cardiac arrest because he didn't have Briar with him? Why did standing here in this room, the room where he had witnessed his mother's death, feel like he was submerged under water and he couldn't breathe? Like his chest was going to explode. If you didn't have a heart…then why the hell was it breaking?

Why was he standing here imagining days filled with darkness? Days without her soft hands touching his skin. Without her looking at him as though he was a person of value. Without her telling him that he mattered? Why was he imagining those things and not the loss of all his political alliances? Because that was all she should mean. It was all she should have ever meant. He should be mounting an attack. Plotting revenge against her for taking herself away from him and ruining his plans. He did not allow such things. He never had.

But the problem was, she was already perfect for him. She didn't even have to try. And without her…without her he was nothing.

He reached into his pocket and pulled out his phone, and without thinking, he dialed Adam's number. Felipe was not the kind of man who depended on the kindness of friends or strangers. Indeed, he had done his very best to never need anyone's kindness. Mostly because he had grown up with none, and had never assumed it would be there when he needed it.

But he needed something now. And he didn't know where else to turn.

"Adam," he said.

"I'm surprised it took you this long to call. Considering your wedding was just dramatically called off."

"Yes. Well. I didn't think I needed anything to deal with that. She's gone. What's done is done. There's nothing I can do to fight that. Nor do I want to. At least, I didn't think so."

"I see. It turns out you're not so happy to have lost your fiancée?"

Felipe felt like he'd been stabbed in the chest. "No. And I'm not thinking about the political ramifications. All I can think of is her. She is... She is impractical for me in every way. She's young. She was innocent." His body warmed just thinking of how far she had come in the past weeks. "She is soft and giving. She is everything I'm not. I shouldn't miss her. I shouldn't want her. And yet..."

"I could have told you that it is a grave mistake to take beautiful young women captive," Adam said, his tone dry. "I have a bit of experience with that."

"You were also the most humorless, angry man I had ever met before Belle came into your life. How did you change? I need to know. I need to know if it's possible."

Adam hesitated for a moment. "I was content to go through my life feeling nothing," he said finally. "The loss of my first wife was more than I could bear. At least, I thought so. I thought I had been damaged beyond the capacity for feeling. I wanted to be. But Belle came softly, and because of that I did not know I needed to arm myself against her. I was so certain that as her captor I held the upper hand. Ultimately, she was the one who captured me. Her love changed me. And the fact that I had to become something different to be worthy of it. It does not just happen as you sit idly by, Felipe. You must choose it. You must choose love instead of darkness. Because that's the only way that it can win in the end. But once you do… Light wins every time. It swallows the darkness whole."

"Perhaps your brand of darkness, Adam. I fear mine might have the power to absorb the sun."

"If that is how you choose to see it, if that is the power you choose to give it, then I believe it. Light and dark exist in the world, Felipe. Good and evil. Love and hate. We must all choose, I suppose, which of those things we give the most power. Which of those things get to carry the most weight. In the end, I chose love. Because anything else was to submit to the unthinkable. A life without Belle. If you can imagine life without Briar, then I suppose you don't need to change at all. But if this present darkness that you're in feels too suffocating, too consuming… Turn on the light, my friend."

"Talia." Queen Amaani walked into the room. It could be no one else. After a week in Verloren she could recognize the other woman by the sound of her footsteps. There was something about the way she glided over the tile, even in heels. She was like an ethereal being.

And Briar looked like her. She was her daughter; there was no denying it.

She was also the daughter of Dr. Robert and Nell Harcourt from New York, who had raised her and loved her and done their best to protect her from a threat they'd had no power against.

Living at the palace in Santa Milagro, then coming

here, truly underscored that fact. How much power the players in this game possessed, that Dr. Harcourt and his wife did not. It was strange, though. That realization didn't make her feel more indebted.

It made her feel…

Well, she felt as if it was the proof of love she'd always been looking for.

It had always been there. She'd just put so many of her own fears up in front of it.

She turned to face the queen, her heart pounding hard. "Briar," she said. "Call me Briar, please?"

The other woman's beautiful face looked shocked, but only for a moment. Then she smoothed it into rather serene calm. "If that's what you prefer, of course."

Briar smiled, knowing the smile looked as sad as she felt inside. "It's more…I've been thinking a lot. About who I am. And what I want. I'm so happy that I've been able get to know you and…and I'm sorry—" her throat tightened up "—I'm sorry that we couldn't have known each other better. I'm sorry that it…is this way. But I was blessed to have a wonderful upbringing with the people you chose to care for me. And…I became the woman they raised me to be. I wanted to be Talia for you. I wanted to please you. But I need to be Briar."

Felipe had always seen her as Briar. Always. Even when she'd told her mother and father to call her Talia, he had known.

He had known long before she had.

Funny how that wretched man could be so insightful about her behavior, and have such a huge blank when it came to his own.

Then the queen did something unexpected. She knelt down in front of Briar, her hands on Briar's lap, her face

full of sadness. "I know. And it is... The reason we chose
the Harcourts was because we had known them for years.
Because we trusted them. Because we knew that they
would help you grow into the woman you were meant
to be. I'm sorry we failed you. I'm sorry you suffered at
the hands of that madman..."

"He's not a madman," she said, surprised by her own
vehemence. "He's...lost. And he's hurt. But he's..." Tears
filled her eyes. "I love him. And I would be with him still
except...it couldn't be like it was. With him convinced
he had forced my hand. With me trying to earn his love.
It has to be different. If he comes for me again, it has to
be because he wants me. Not because he wants a wife he
thinks will make him look good. And I need to go with
him because I love him. Not because he kidnapped me
from a hospital."

The queen's eyebrows shot up. "From a hospital?"

Briar sighed. "It's a long story."

The queen rose to her feet and sat in the chair next to
Briar. Then she snapped her elegant fingers. A servant
appeared. "Tea," she said. Then she turned her focus
back to Briar. "I have time for long stories. The two of
us have much catching up to do, Briar."

CHAPTER THIRTEEN

FELIPE HAD NEVER imagined coming to Verloren. Especially not without armed guards. Or an entire battalion. Not considering the relations between the two countries. It was one of the many reasons he had wanted Briar in the first place. She was a convenient human shield. One that forced the nations to be friendly.

But he was coming now as an enemy, with no defenses. With nothing. Nothing except a whole lot of darkness inside him that he wanted so desperately to shine a light on.

Briar's light.

Whether he deserved it or not, that was what he was here for.

He didn't expect a hero's welcome, but he didn't expect to be put in chains the moment he showed up at the palace, either. And yet he was. He also allowed it, because the last thing he could afford was the kind of scandal that would erupt if he committed an act of violence in a foreign palace.

And he also couldn't afford to do anything that Briar might disapprove of.

Especially not with her father, the king, looking on as he was led into the palace throne room.

"King Felipe," he said. "It is a surprise to see you. You will forgive the precautions. But last time you were around a member of my family without chains, you took her against her will."

He did not bother to correct the king by saying that last time he had been around the man's daughter he'd been the one to tell her not to return. And that before that she'd been in his arms—in his bed—willingly.

Felipe didn't want to die. Not today.

Perhaps after he met with Briar, perhaps if she rejected him. But not before he had the chance to try.

"I welcomed you to my palace without chains," Felipe pointed out.

"I was also invited. What is your business here?"

"I'm here to see the princess."

"You're here to claim a debt that isn't yours to claim, and was never meant to extend to my daughter," the older man said, standing. "I refuse. Even if it means war. I should have done that years ago."

"I am not here to claim her, as a payment or otherwise. I am here to speak to her. I'm here to tell her…"

"Here to tell me what?"

He looked toward the doors that led in deeper to the palace and saw Briar standing there. It was strange to see her dressed so casually. Wearing just dark jeans and a gray T-shirt, her hair loose and curly, her face void of makeup.

Strange, and yet she was even more beautiful to him now than she had been in the most beautiful of ball gowns. Because this wasn't a memory. This was now. She was here standing before him, and he had made a decision.

That made her the most beautiful she'd ever been to

him. It made this the most beautiful moment, in a world that had—to this point—been mostly darkness and pain for him.

"I am in chains," he said, lifting his wrists to show her.

"Oh, well…good. Now you'll have an idea of what it's like to be held against your will." She crossed her arms, cocking her hip to the side, her expression serene.

"Is there a chance, as I am in chains, I might speak to you alone? I can't do anything in this state, after all."

Her father's expression turned sharp. "Absolutely not."

Briar held up her hand. "Yes. I need to speak with him. I need to hear what he has to say."

The old king paused then looked at his guards. "Let us go. Briar, if you have need of us, you know what to do."

She nodded. "Thank you."

Once the king and his henchmen had exited the room, Felipe turned his focus back to Briar. "He called you Briar."

"Yes. I'm not Talia. I…explained that to them yesterday. I need to be…me. And that's Briar. Briar Harcourt. It doesn't mean I can't visit here. And I would like to get to know them. But…I'm me."

He knew what it meant. She didn't have to explain. Because he knew her. He could honestly say he had never known anyone else quite as well. And certainly no one had known him.

"Briar." He just wanted to say her name. Wanted to watch her respond to him. To his words. To his voice. Wanted to confirm that she wasn't neutral to him. No. No, she was not. It took three steps for him to close the space between them and when he did, he looped his arms around her, trapping her in the chain, pulling her up against him.

"I'm not here to steal you," he said, leaning in, pressing his lips to hers. "But I am here for you."

"You said…" Her voice wobbled.

"That I would not claim you. Not for revenge. Not for payment. But I want you." He drew her even closer, wrapping the chain around his wrists to make it so she couldn't pull away. "I *need* you."

"Why do I feel like you're trying to take me captive again?" she whispered, her dark eyes glittering.

"Impossible," he said. "I'm the one in chains. I suspect I have been for a very long time. But it took the desire to be free for me to truly recognize my limitations. When I wished so much I could hold you, but knew I could not because it would only harm us both. Because…because if I am in chains then holding you means having you in them, as well, and you were right. It would have only destroyed us both. That has long been my fear. That I destroy, rather than build. That I am my father's son, and I can only break things, even the things I love."

"And you're holding me in chains now," she pointed out.

"Yes, but this is literal, because I want you against me. Touching me. The other was metaphorical."

"I see," she said, the side of her mouth quirking upward. "But none of it matters if you haven't found the key."

"To my chains? Oh, I have. The metaphorical chains. Not these. Your father will have to release me from these."

She lifted her hands, taking hold of his face. "Unless you're going to tell me how you found the key, you can shut up."

He took that opportunity to wrap the chains yet another time around his wrist, hauling her closer as he dipped his head and claimed her mouth with his. When they parted, they were both breathing hard.

"You," he ground out. "You're the key, Briar. To all of this. To me."

"I am?"

"Yes," he said. "You. Not as a princess, but as a woman. You made me see...you made me see for the first time in years. You shone a light on my darkness. And even more than allowing me to see, you saw me. You saw me and you wouldn't allow me to hide."

"You saw me," she said, the words husky. "You made me stronger. You made me fight."

"It was in you all along," he said. "That fight. You just had to come up against a dragon to find it."

She smiled. "I like that."

"And I love you." The words scraped his throat raw. He couldn't remember if he'd ever spoken them before. He didn't think he had. "All my childhood I'd been too bound up in fear and abuse to...to feel much of anything. I dismissed it. I dismissed it as something that didn't matter because I didn't truly understand. I didn't know what it meant to love someone, or to have them love you. I didn't understand the power of it. I thought...I thought that perhaps my mother's death was something I could have fixed. If I had done more. If I had been better."

"No," she said, pressing her fingertips to his lips. "No. You were a little boy, Felipe. Of course you couldn't have stopped it."

"It felt like it was me," he said, his voice strained. "That I was the one who broke her."

"No, Felipe. It was him."

"I know. I know now. There was only ever one person who could have stopped the hell we lived in, and that was my father. And that small thing. That thing he taught me meant nothing…love. It would have healed so much, Briar. If he would have had it for me, for my mother. For anyone but himself. Love is not a negligible thing. I have come to believe that it is the only thing."

"I love you, Felipe." She smiled at him. And it was like the sun had risen after the darkest night, shining a light in the hidden corners of his soul.

He kissed her again, and he felt something lift away from him. A weight, a darkness that had rested upon him for longer than he could remember. He had tried to banish it with anger, with hate. With vengeance. But nothing had taken it from him. Until this. Until her love.

Love was stronger.

That was how the princess slew the dragon. Not with a sword. Not with a magic spell.

But with love.

And they lived happily ever after…

* * * * *

If you enjoyed
THE PRINCE'S STOLEN VIRGIN
by Maisey Yates
make sure you read the first part of her trilogy
ONCE UPON A SEDUCTION…
THE PRINCE'S CAPTIVE VIRGIN
Available now!

And keep an eye out for the final installment,
Rafe and Charlotte's story
Coming October 2017!

In the meantime why not explore another
trilogy by Maisey Yates?
HEIRS BEFORE VOWS
THE SPANIARD'S PREGNANT BRIDE
THE PRINCE'S PREGNANT MISTRESS
THE ITALIAN'S PREGNANT VIRGIN
Available now!

MILLS & BOON®

EXCLUSIVE EXTRACT

Natasha Pellegrini and Matteo Manaserro's reunion
catches them both in a potent mix of emotion, and they
surrender to their explosive passion. Natasha was a virgin
until Matteo's touch branded her as his and when Matteo
discovers Natasha is pregnant, he's intent on claiming his
baby. Except he hasn't bargained on their insatiable
chemistry binding them together so completely!

Read on for a sneak preview of Michelle Smart's book
CLAIMING HIS ONE-NIGHT BABY
The second part of her Bound to a Billionaire trilogy

'For better or worse we're going to be tied together by our
child for the rest of our lives and the only way we're going
to get through it is by always being honest with each other.
We will argue and disagree but you must always speak the
truth to me.'

Natasha fought to keep her feet grounded and her limbs
from turning into fondue but it was a fight she was losing,
Matteo's breath warm on her face, his thumb gently moving
on her skin but scorching it, the heat from his body almost
penetrating her clothes, heat crawling through her, pooling
in her most intimate place.

His scent was right there too, filling every part of her, and
she wanted to bury her nose into his neck and inhale him.

She'd kissed him without any thought, a desperate
compulsion to touch him and comfort him flooding her, and
then the fury had struck from nowhere, all her private thoughts
about the direction he'd taken his career in converging to
realise he'd thrown it all away in the pursuit of riches.

And now she wanted to kiss him again.

As if he could sense the need inside her, he brought his mouth close to hers but not quite touching, the promise of a kiss.

'And now I will ask you something and I want complete honesty,' he whispered, the movement of his words making his lips dance against hers like a breath.

The fluttering of panic sifted into the compulsive desire. She hated lies too. She never wanted to tell another, especially not to him. But she had to keep her wits about her because there were things she just could not tell because no matter what he said about lies always being worse, sometimes it was the truth that could destroy a life.

But, God, how could she think properly when her head was turning into candyfloss at his mere touch?

His other hand trailed down her back and clasped her bottom to pull her flush to him. Her abdomen clenched to feel his erection pressing hard against her lower stomach. His lips moved lightly over hers, still tantalising her with the promise of his kiss. 'Do you want me to let you go?'

Her hands that she'd clenched into fists at her sides to stop from touching him back unfurled themselves and inched to his hips.

The hand stroking her cheek moved round her head and speared her hair. 'Tell me.' His lips found her exposed neck and nipped gently at it. 'Do you want me to stop?'

'Matteo...' Finally, she found her voice.

'Yes, *bella*?'

'Don't stop.'

Don't miss
CLAIMING HIS ONE-NIGHT BABY
By Michelle Smart

Available September 2017
www.millsandboon.co.uk